# Judgement

## The Revelation Trilogy
### Book 2

T. E. Burrell

Judgement is a work of fiction. All of the names, characters, locations, and events are products of the author's imagination or are used fictitiously. Any resemblance to actual persons, places, or events is entirely coincidental.

ISBN: 979-8-9914559-1-6

# DEDICATION

The Revelation Trilogy is dedicated to the two women who made it possible.

My mother Mickey, FORCED me to read for an hour every day during my summer break between first and second grade. It started an obsession that I am forever grateful for.

My wife Becky supplied an amazing level of patience and understanding along the journey. Those who know me well can attest this is no small feat. Without her advice and support this story would still be rolling around in my head all by itself.

# CONTENTS

# ACKNOWLEDGMENTS

My thanks to Jordan for his insightful feedback, questions, ideas, and encouragement during the writing of this trilogy. His developmental editing was incredibly helpful.

Thanks also to Jess and Emmaleigh for their help with the cover art. Their advice, energy, and creativity is greatly appreciated by someone who is significantly artwork challenged.

I

Judgement

# CHAPTER 1

# SEARCH PARTY

G rammy was worried. Tee didn't show up on the fifth day as promised. That wasn't like him. When the poor boy had shown up on her doorstep last week he had been more distraught than she had ever seen him. He was so overwhelmed by trauma and guilt that she tried to get him to delay his hunting trip. She thought a few days talking it out would be good for him. Tee told her he had to get by himself to sort it all out. This was how Tee solved personal problems his whole life. So, she was hopeful he would find the healing he needed in the woods. He promised her he would be back by the fifth day. He said he would spend a couple of days with her before having to report back to the Guard. She remembered their last conversation. "Where are you going to be?"

"Not telling Grammy. If you don't know they can't get it out of you," Tee said.

"What's wrong with you? Somebody ought to know in case you do something stupid or clumsy out there. God knows it wouldn't be the first time," she said. That actually made him chuckle, a sound that warmed her heart after an entire day of sorrow and tears.

"Sorry but I need the time alone. Ansen and Diana will come find me if they know where to look," Tee said.

Grammy knew something had happened that Tee hadn't told her about. While they were both distraught about Tia, he seemed downright guilty about it. He also said very little about either Ansen or Diana. That was unusual. Tee tended to be on the private side. He tended not to say bad things about people. There was more to this story.

Late in the afternoon on the sixth day Arti, Hugh, Ansen, Pete, and Diana all arrived. Instead of going home they had all shown up on Grammy's front porch.

Arti started the conversation with, "where is Tee mom?"

"He left here six days ago and was supposed to be back yesterday afternoon, latest," Grammy said with concern in her voice.

"Where was he going?" Diana asked.

"He wouldn't tell me. Said he didn't want you or Ansen to find him until he was ready to be found. That was cryptic so I tried to find out what happened between the three of you that had him so insistent," Grammy said with a hint of accusation in her voice.

There was dead silence for an uncomfortable amount of time until Ansen spoke up, "It's my fault Grammy. I told Tee at Tia's funeral that I blamed him for her death. I had asked him to look after her on the Wall. I told him she was dead because he failed to do that," Ansen said with tears forming in his eyes. "I know Tee loves Tia as much as I do. It was cruel and selfish to take out my anguish on Tee. I just hope he'll forgive me."

Grammy just glared at him for a few moments. Then her face softened and with compassion in her voice said, "he will Ansen, he will. The one time he did talk about you was to complement your bravery on the Wall. Evidently you fought beside his friend Jay who had good things to say about him. He also said you were as good a brother to him as you've always been to Pete." Ansen turned bright red looking completely embarrassed and Pete just looked down at the ground. Perhaps I shouldn't have said that, thought Grammy. But Ansen knows better than to say something like that. He needs to be called out on it. The two of them are like brothers.

Turning towards Diana she asked bluntly, "why was he

worried about you Diana?"

"I don't know Grammy," Diana said earnestly but with something held back.

There was way more to that story. But now wasn't the time to get it out of her. Diana was like a granddaughter to Grammy. She hated pushing her in front of everyone, but her anxiety over Tee overrode any concerns of making Diana uncomfortable. Diana was definitely holding something back. It wasn't like her to lie, even by omission.

Arti spoke up. "It's time to organize a search. I'll go down to the Sheriff and see if he can help us drum up some volunteers. Most people are still making their way back from the Wall. Some decided to help the Eureka farmers with the planting. God knows they are stretched. We aren't going to get the number of people we would usually get for something like this."

"Maybe we could get the Guard to help. I'm sure they would be interested in helping us find him," Diana offered.

"That's a good idea. Hugh, could Pete go back down the falls and find the Guard scout team we saw there yesterday?" Arti asked.

"Of course. We need to find our boy," Hugh said. "Pete, turn around and head down the falls this afternoon. Stay with your aunt and uncle tonight in Apple River. As soon as it's light tomorrow go look for that scout team. Tell them Tee is missing. Diana, you go hunting with Tee, where should we start?"

"Lets go into town and ask around. Maybe someone saw which direction he was headed in. If we know that I can make a better guess." Diana answered.

Later that day Diana suggested they wait for the Scout Team because she thought she knew where Tee went. She explained her theory to Arti, "Steve at the general store said Tee bought bread and fruit to take with him. Enough for four or five days he thought. He noticed him heading in the direction of the east side trail which means he's probably over on that side somewhere. Tee won't kill anything he's not planning on eating, so it's a minimum of small game. That means he'll have lots of time on his hands with nothing to do. He's not a person who's going to sit around," Diana said.

"He hasn't stayed in one place since he could crawl," Arti confirmed with a sad smile.

"He likes to explore so I think he went somewhere he hasn't fully explored. That eliminates anything that can be done in a day trip and most of the east side. We talked once about taking a few days and exploring the north end of the east side. There are a couple of small valleys up there. They are really remote, and he wouldn't run into anyone up there. Just the sort of place he would go," Diana said.

Pete showed up late in the afternoon with Scout Team 5. "We came as soon as Pete found us," Staff Sergeant Willis said to Arti. "Tee was supposed to join our team on his next cycle. We've already done some training with him. I guess I'm telling you this because we consider him one of our own. If he can be found, we'll find him."

"Thank you Sergeant. If you need anything just let me know. This is Diana." Arti said motioning over to her. "She has spent many hours hunting with Tee and will go along with you. She knows his habits and his preferences, which might be helpful."

"A pleasure to meet you Diana." Sergeant Willis studied her for a few moments and then said, "Weren't you one of the hunters who discovered the GEMs and then helped drive them off the cliffs?"

Diana blushed and simply said, "yes."

"Sergeant Glenn is quite the fan," Sergeant Willis said with a grin to the amused chuckles of the rest of his team.

Diana's blush turned scarlet.

Noticing her embarrassment, he respectfully said, "I'm sorry. I didn't mean to embarrass you Diana." Sergeant Willis smile faded, and he continued, "we're all deeply appreciative of what you've done here in Apple Valley and at the Wall. Everyone in the Guard loves it when they have Apple Valley archer support." He glanced over to include Arti in his appreciation. Willis then sighed and said, "it's already close to sunset so let's meet in the town square before first light. We need to be able to look for signs and can't do that in the dark. This is Corporal Walker. He's the best tracker in the Guard. In fact, he's the one who trains new recruits. Tell him everything you know about Tee's habits and tendencies when he's hiking. Does he go off trail often, if so, what draws him off? Favorite places to stop and rest, things like that."

"Thank you," Arti said sweeping her hand to encompass the entire scout team." I can't tell you how much I appreciate your help with this," Arti added catching all of them with her intense eyes.

"He's one of our own ma'am. We'll look until we find him," Sergeant Willis said.

After most of a day hiking up the east side of Apple Valley they reached the first of the smaller northeast valley trails. Sergeant Willis called for a halt and motioned Walker towards the trail. Walker was tall and rangy. He seemed to blend into the environment moving smoothly and easily. He nodded his head and started up the trail carefully staying off the main path and looking intently from side to side. He soon disappeared around a bend.

Thirty minutes later he came back and said, "there isn't any recent activity on this trail. They told me in town that it rained two weeks ago, just before Tee left. The trail only has animal tracks on it. Let's go look at the next spot."

Four hours later Walker strove up the next trail and came back quickly, excitement clear on his face. "There is one set of tracks going up, and none coming back," he said. "It's a Guard issue boot and on the small side. Give me 10 minutes then follow me up the trail at a slow pace." And with that he disappeared with his long strides up the steep forest trail leading alongside a rushing stream to the valley above.

Just after sunset Walker appeared coming quickly back down the trail towards them with a bow, arrows, and backpack. Diana blurted out, "those are Tee's! Is he OK?"

"Don't know Diana. I searched the general area around where I found these and didn't find Tee," Walker said. "Staff Sergeant, would you come with me. I need to show you something. Sorry but everyone else needs to stay put. I don't want anything disturbed until I can look the area over in full light tomorrow."

When they returned Sergeant Willis looked grave. He turned to one of the scouts and said. "Hollings, go find Master Sergeant Ricks and tell him Tee is missing. Tell him Walker found something unusual connected to Tee's disappearance and I'm requesting his presence. Tell him we're going to search this Valley until he shows up. And Hollings, go as fast as you can." Willis looked over at Diana and could see the barely contained anxiety. He took a deep breath, let it out, and then said, "Griff will probably kill me for telling you what we found. Can you keep what I tell you secret? That means from everyone."

"Yes." Diana said with her heart in her throat.

"Tell her Walker," Willis said.

"I think he was ambushed and taken somewhere. There isn't any blood or even signs of a fight. He appears to have just collapsed in the middle of the trail. The other signs are hard to believe. Surrounding where the person fell are a number of adolescent sized footprints with unusual soles. Strides are consistent with someone not fully grown. It looks like they picked Tee up, tried to carry him, gave up, and then dragged him to a nearby clearing. All the signs disappear in the middle of that clearing. It's like he just vanished," Walker said, clearly troubled to be telling her this.

Diana was stunned, she didn't know what to say. Then she blurted out in disbelief, "he's been kidnapped?"

"It looks that way. It certainly wasn't GEMs if that's any consolation," Sergeant Willis said. "I have no idea what to make of it. I'm hoping Ricks can help us sort this out. We will do an exhaustive search of the valley and make sure he isn't here somewhere. Would you stay and help?"

"You don't have to ask; I'm staying and looking for him regardless of whether you want me to or not," Diana said as she fought to control her emotions.

"We're glad to have your help Diana," Willis said with a gentle voice and troubled look.

Diana might be calm on the outside, but inside she was screaming. In a way it might be good news. She was worried he had run into GEMs or fallen off a cliff. She had even harbored thoughts of him taking his own life. Tee was the last person she thought might do that. But, he had undergone a tremendous amount of trauma in a short period of time and that can do strange things to a person. Diana was very angry with herself. She should have gone to Tee when Ansen lost his temper. Ansen wasn't the one who needed her in that situation. Tee was. They all thought of Tee as tougher than anyone. Tee was always OK. It would be her life's tragedy if she were never able to apologize and tell Tee how she really felt about him.

# CHAPTER 2

# CONFRONTATION

G riff walked into the Blue Heron Tavern and sat down heavily in a chair across from Del. He had an angry stern expression on his face.

"What, no hello, no insults," Del said trying to lighten the mood.

"Hello," Griff said stiffly. Then he just continued to look sternly at him.

Del hesitated and then with concern in his voice said, "I heard Tee is missing."

Griff continued to glare at him for a few moments longer and then asked in a stern and threatening voice, "what are you hiding?"

Del replied with both hands raised and surprise written all over it, "what do you mean?"

Griff's frown deepened. "I've known for a while you're hiding something. Your engineering department is especially fishy," Griff said accusingly.

"Why do you say that?" Del replied looking down into his whiskey.

"You send out a new 'military history' student every few years to learn about Guard tactics and strategies. They're always young, smart, and attempting to hide their involvement in your engineering department. When I ask what they want to learn from the Guard they give me the same answer. The same EXACT answer. It's clear they've been coached on what to say. If I try and dig deeper into their objectives, they get hesitant, cagy, and fiend confusion." Griff hesitated a moment and continued, "If I wasn't in charge of Guard training and naturally paranoid I never would have gotten suspicious. Once my suspicions were raised I noticed other peculiarities. For instance, engineering technologies seem to flow out of the university cleanly and systematically. It's not as messy as I would expect new discoveries to be. I can also tell when you're not being completely forthright with your answers to my questions."

Del continued to examine his whiskey and did not answer.

Griff sighed, let out a deep breath and said, "our scout teams are very good at tracking. Most people don't know that GEMs get past the cliff forts and into the wilderness occasionally. This is mostly a problem in the mountains on the western side above Landfall and Eureka Valleys. As you know a full-scale invasion was recently attempted in Apple Valley. Our scout teams are the ones who hunt them down. We keep quiet about it because we don't want people to panic. When Tee went missing we were able to identify his last location and were surprised by what we found. Based on evidence at the site, which I have seen with my own eyes, children snatched him. They tried to carry him and failed so they dragged him to a nearby clearing. From there he magically disappeared." Griff hesitated and staring aggressively at Del said, "I'm convinced you know something about his disappearance."

Del was rarely stunned into silence. He started to reply, stopped, hesitated some more, then finally looked up from his whiskey and said, "give me a day or two and I'll tell you what I can."

Griff's eyes bored right through him as he said, "a missing member of the Guard is involved. I can't let this go. I know you, so I'm sure you have your reasons for hiding whatever it is you're hiding. But one way or another, I'm going to get to the bottom of this." Having said what he needed to say, Griff abruptly stood up and walked out of the tavern.

Del took an especially deep breath and let it out slowly. As he sat there he transitioned from panicked to resigned. Once again he was left with lots to think about after meeting with Griff. Damn him, why can't we just meet for dinner and have a pleasant conversation?

CHAPTER 3

# THE COMMITTEE

While Del was waiting for the other Committee members he reflected on how Pacifica had gotten into such a precarious position. Barlow was extremely irritating, but his accusation of a manipulated history was true. The official history of Pacifica was a lie. Barlow was clever in uncovering it. But he was entirely wrong about the purpose of the lie. There was a good reason. It was a life-or-death reason. The irony was that a group of committed pacifists, with the best of intentions, created two of the most warlike cultures ever known. While the people of the peninsula could argue they were defending themselves, they were killing and being killed by other intelligent beings on a monumental scale.

The original emigration plan was to permanently separate from the rest of humankind. The goal was to live an isolated and peaceful life. After a long search, sabotage marooned them in a stable orbit around a planet presenting significant terraforming challenges. It was a massive planet. Gravity was higher than humans were accustomed to. It also had a slightly more extreme axis tilt than Earths. This meant it had larger extremes of seasonal heat and cold than the environment humans are best suited for. There was a single long narrow peninsula on the north end of the smaller of the two continents. It was situated near the equator with deep temperate oceans surrounding it. This kept the temperature extremes of summer and winter reasonably regulated. It was the only location on the planet that could possibly support unmodified humans. One of the main motivations for permanent separation from the rest of humanity was moral abhorrence with genocide. That it was being carried out on those possessing engineered genetic alterations was not a justification for this horror. The so-called Mutant Wars in Earths solar system had just been lost by the genetically impure. The victors were sure of their moral superiority. They were diligent in a brutal quest to ensure genetically engineered modified humans, or GEMs, would disappear forever.

Earth had developed a standard colonization process after decades of trial and error. Triple redundant starships had been shown to have many advantages. By keeping the three starships coordinated but isolated from one another the ravages of disease and societal dysfunction could be confined. You might lose one of the ships, but experience had shown you were unlikely to lose more than that. Spare parts and expertise could be shared as long as physical contact was kept sterile and communication was limited to specific objectives. The other requirement was locking down language and culture. Humans were combative enough without the challenge of navigating multiple dynamic cultures. For this reason, there was a right way and a wrong way to speak and act. When the three starships recombined, people had to be able to communicate and blend back into a single culture.

Not all of the Pacifica colonists were genetically pure humans. This was the genesis of the false history. Ship 2 had smuggled onboard a population of GEMs who had escaped capture towards the end of the Mutant Wars. These GEMs were a team of scientists with a pacifist bent. This GEM population had minimal modifications and were visibly indistinguishable from unmodified humans. Only extensive genetic testing could uncover the truth. Unfortunately, extensive genetic testing was a requirement for all citizens after the war. The moral alignment, indistinguishable modifications, and addition of unique and valuable skills were too appealing for the inhabitants of Ship 2 to ignore. They felt they could not allow these scientists to be handed over for genocide.

The three-ship alliance first broke apart over the strategy of colonizing Pacifica. A planet named in honor of the colonists' intentions. After decades in space, Ship 2 was primarily populated by GEMs. The populations of Ships 1 and 3 were unmodified. Both groups agreed that some modification was likely needed to ensure survival. An analysis suggested a 70% probability of success if they confined themselves to the peninsula and avoided modification. This was considered dangerously low. Ship 2 proposed massive genetic modifications to enable colonization of the whole planet. Ships 1 and 3 wanted to limit changes to just those calculated to be probable by natural micro-evolution. This would still limit them to the relatively mild environment of the peninsula. If done properly it would allow the modifications to potentially remain hidden if the rest of humanity discovered them.

They finally agreed to disagree. A compatible middle ground was found. They were the descendants of pacifists after all. There was an agreement to separate into two colonies. Ships 1 and 3 would own the peninsula and Ship 2 the rest of the habitable parts of the world.

Harmony and cooperation only lasted for a single generation. The second generation of genetically altered offspring of Ship 2 suddenly murdered what was left of the original Ship 2 colonists and attacked those living on the peninsula. War was sudden, brutal, and devastating for both races. In the end all three spaceships were destroyed and both races plunged into an agrarian state fighting to survive.

What the peninsula kept secret was that it retained much of its technological knowledge. Information hidden away in caves was waiting for society to recover enough to be able to invest the time and energy needed to make use of it. The crisis struck just as that had begun to be possible. Their sector had been discovered by the Commonwealth and other solar systems were being colonized. By sheer luck, the radio operator on duty that day decided to stay silent when local microwave radio traffic was first received. Their freedom and likely their lives had been saved by that decision. It didn't take long to realize the danger they were in. Listening to their new neighbors they learned that the violently anti-GEM society they escaped had turned into a sprawling authoritarian government spread across the universe. This Commonwealth was fanatically committed to maintaining true human purity. This was when the Committee was first formed. They took steps to create a false history and over many generations aggressively erased all traces of evidence contradicting that history. Oral histories were the most problematic. Traces of those written in private journals and stored with records in small town parishes were what Barlow had uncovered.

It was common knowledge that a system of caves existed beneath the university. This cave system was owned by the university and used for natural refrigeration, storing records, and archiving artifacts from the original colonists. What was known to a select few was the existence of a carefully hidden and extensive tunnel system branching off from it. This tunnel system had been carved out of the rock by the original colonists for use as a bunker. It was to a conference room in that tunnel system that the Committee convened.

There were four members of the Committee. Professor Delvin Dacy, Dr. Dorothy Espers, Kevin Wise, and President Jennifer Malrey.

"Thank you for coming so quickly. I apologize for the last-minute request and appreciate the difficulties it presented," Del said looking around the table. "This emergency meeting is to discuss the rapidly deteriorating situation at the Wall."

"Has something changed since the last meeting." Asked Jennifer with a worried expression.

"We've intercepted more communications from the survey ship orbiting the planet," Del said. "They continue to report that the GEMs have retreated as relayed in our last meeting. But they are not dispersing. This is new behavior. The survey ship crew is communicating to A27 that it's just a matter of time before the GEMs regroup. They expect the next attack to break into the peninsula and wipe us out."

"Remind me how the Commonwealth is structured and why their laws allow for the genocide of true humans by GEMs?" the President asked. "I'm sorry to drag you all through this but as you know I was just elected and am new to all of this."

"Not a problem Ms. President," Del said.

"Please call me Jennifer for these Committee meetings. We are all tied together closely in our struggle and formality will just get in the way," she declared.

"Ok, done Jennifer. Everything I tell you is based on listening and not being able to ask questions. It means everything I say on this subject is unverified speculation. It is speculation based on lots of intercepted communications over the years, but speculation none the less," Del said. "Our understanding is that the Commonwealth is motivated by tax revenue growth and a monopoly on technology-based manufacturing. They accomplish growth by colonizing new planets and incorporating previous expeditions, like ours. They set up one planet per sector to take in raw materials produced by the colonies in that sector and turn them into trade goods. We are in Sector 27. The name for the Commonwealth owned planet in this sector is A27. The A stands for Administrative.

We believe they base their economic model on the British Empire of the 18th century. Recognizing that the British system fell apart because of colonial rebellion they have devised a system to eliminate that threat. They control trade and technology-based manufacturing by keeping the colonies at a pre-industrial level. The colonies supply raw materials, agricultural products, and cheap labor-based manufacturing. Commonwealth corporations and citizens get obscenely wealthy.

By completely controlling transportation they control interplanetary and intersectional trade. This is their sole source of tax revenue. Since they transport everything it is extremely easy to administer and impossible to avoid. They don't appear to bother controlling politics on individual colony planets. As long as tax revenues and raw materials are flowing they don't get involved. It does appear they sometimes intentionally create conflict between planets if they believe they can increase tax revenues or their own manufacturing output. To effectively manage such a large number of diversely located planets they have divided it into sectors defined by permanent wormhole boundaries. Each sector has a Governor whose authority is absolute as long as the Commonwealths Edicts are being observed. We have reason to suspect our sector's bureaucracy is corrupt. We don't know if corruption is limited to our sector or a widespread attribute of the Commonwealth.

One of the Commonwealths Edicts is that civilizations of true humans in a pre-industrial state with only first-generation warfare capabilities are to be left alone. Evidently they are very interested in societal evolution and want to study it. All colony planets are restricted to first generation warfare and the Commonwealth is brutal in enforcing this Edict. They keep subject planets at a technological level that eliminates their ability to revolt. We know that whole planets have been destroyed or their populations enslaved for hiding even mildly sophisticated weapons or violating any of the technology Edicts. As you know another of their Edicts is to eliminate all GEM races as they are discovered. However, it appears that the Edict to leave true humans alone extends to the current protection of GEMs on our planet. We've intercepted a communication from the survey ship stating that if the GEMs wipe us out it validates their belief in the prohibition of genetic alterations. It's a self-serving justification for their system of genocide. Our belief is that once we use second generation warfare or cross the boundary into an industrial state the Commonwealth will invade. We don't know if they will install their own government or hand us over to one of the other colonies in our sector. Slavery is common on Arista and our guess is that we would be placed under their control. On the other hand, if the GEMs wipe us out the Commonwealth will come in. They would cleanse the planet of GEMs and strip Pacifica of its natural resources."

"Why are we only worried about Arista?" Jennifer asked.

"I would say we are more worried about Arista than the others. Arista was originally formed with a benevolent dictator advised by a senate comprised of citizens. Citizens are the descendants of the original wealthy families that funded the colonization. Everyone else came with indentured servant status and that class system hasn't changed much in almost a millennium. Over several generations, the benevolence disappeared and an obsession with ancient Rome and its Emperors emerged. They endorse the idea that the citizen class is superior to all other classes. That slavery is the rightful position of the lowest class. They conspire to take over the sector and the Commonwealth doesn't seem to be interested in stopping them. They may even have some level of support. There are indications that Commonwealth tax revenues can somehow be increased in that circumstance.

The other significant planet is Liberty. They have a constitutional monarchy with strong protections for their people. It's similar to our belief in the natural rights of humans. This extends to abhorrence for the condition of slavery. The advisory body for their monarch can only make suggestions for new laws, taxes, and declarations of war. Amendments to the constitution must be proposed by their House of Lords but can only be approved by their king or queen. All decision making outside of constitutional declarations and protections are completely within the authority of the king. Currently Liberty is embroiled in a civil war over succession. A younger brother is attempting to overthrow the succession and take the crown. This came soon after a long war of unification where the current kingdom defeated the two other kingdoms on the planet. They definitely have some similarities to the class system on Arista. But each member of society is free and has rights.

The Commonwealths modeling of 18th century British Empire might explain the societal class structure similarities between the two colonies.

Outside of the obligatory Commonwealth planet which manages the bureaucracy of the sector, there are seven additional colonies. They are all relatively poor agricultural societies and pose no threat.

Jennifer took a deep breath and said, "well hearing it again doesn't make it any better. It certainly explains the extensive efforts we take to slow down innovation and hide what technology we do have."

"And we need to hide that technology regardless of how this plays out," Del said. "If they discover we have been hiding industrial technology they will accuse us of avoiding Commonwealth taxes. If they discover we are hiding next generation weapons, no matter how insignificant, they will consider us to be in rebellion. Either way, the best case for our population is enslavement. If they discover our genetically engineered modifications we're all dead."

"The good news is that only Committee members know we have been genetically modified. We know slavers have kidnapped numerous individuals from Pacifica over the years. Given that some of the planet's population is GEM they would have done extensive genetic testing on the captives. We assume they have not discovered our modifications, because if they had we wouldn't be sitting here," Dorothy added. "It was brilliant to do the original modifications in a way that probabilistically fits with natural micro-evolution induced by selective breeding. We have a simple solution to keep this hidden forever."

Only Dorothy would refer to all past and present Committee members committing suicide as a 'simple solution' Del thought smiling to himself. "Back to the purpose of our meeting," Del said looking around the table. "I believe it's just a matter of time before the GEM's get past the Wall and threaten the Landfall Dam. We still have a few tricks up our sleeves that don't involve second generation warfare, but we are running out of time. With that in mind I have a proposal for the Committee," Del concluded.

"Is this proposal within the scope of our current powers," Jennifer asked.

"Yes, it resides within the secret addendum to the constitution that formed this Committee," Del replied. "My proposal is that we add the military to the Committee. In my opinion Master Sergeant Ricks, Griff, is the best choice. The reason for this addition is to get ready for the day we have to use second generation warfare to hold off the GEMs. That will be the day we effectively announce ourselves to the Commonwealth."

"That will mean the GEM race will be eliminated by the Commonwealth," Dorothy said with her bland expression.

If you looked closely you could see her eyes were slightly dilated, which Del now understood meant she was troubled. Thank you Phyllis Del thought. "I think we are all in agreement we will avoid this until our survival is threatened. A last option," Del said.

"Ok, let's vote first on whether to add a military member to the Committee. If it passes we can discuss who should be asked to take on that role," Jennifer said. "Kevin?"

"I vote yes. There aren't any financial implications, and I agree with Del's points,"

Kevin was the finance minister for Pacifica. His responsibility was ensuring all government spending fit within the balanced budget requirement in the constitution. The only exception to this restriction were materials needed for war. Everyone knew the government could come in at any time and confiscate. They would get reimbursed, but that reimbursement had to fit within the balanced budget guidelines. No government spending was possible without Kevins approval. His role on the Committee was as secretary and financial controller. He had proven to be excellent at hiding the funds they needed to enact their decisions. It was a good thing for Pacifica he was a public servant because he would be filthy rich and useless to them otherwise.

"Dorothy?"

"It's a logical move, yes. This should have been proposed sooner. We don't have margin for error," Dorothy said with her deadpan expression. Del smiled to himself once more recalling Phyliss's advice. While Dorothy was bluntly calling out the error in not tabling this sooner, it was just an observation not a personal attack.

"And Del?"

"Yes."

"The proposal to add the military to the Committee passes unanimously."

"Let's move to who we should add. Why are you proposing Master Sergeant Ricks? Isn't the CGG in charge of the Guard?" Jennfier asked.

"The CGG would be the natural choice. He's an excellent administrator and highly respected by the Guard. But he's mired in tradition and doesn't think outside his own experience and the historical record. The more important point is that Griff is the real leader of the Guard. They all follow his lead on important matters. Even the CGG. Griff is intelligent, creative, open minded, and not reluctant to collaborate as part of a team," Del explained.

"I know both Griff and the CGG well," Dorothy said. "I agree that Griff is the best choice."

"Any other nominations?" Jennifer asked. After a few moments of silence, she said, "If there are no other nominations then let's vote. Kevin, we already have Del and Dorothy's votes. Do you agree or want to discuss further?"

"I don't know either candidate, but I trust the combined judgement of those who do. I vote yes." Kevin said.

"It's decided. We will invite Griff to join the Committee with the responsibility of leading military matters with a full vote on all decisions. I'm sure you all realize this means we can now be dead locked on decisions. Per the Committee charter the President facilitates the Committee and only votes to break a tie," Jennifer said. "Del, since you know him best would you deliver the invitation and bring him up to speed?" Then hesitating she continued with a flat smile, "I hope he's not as scary as he appears."

Del chuckled and said, "he will be very respectful Jennifer. I think you'll like him once you get to know him." Del had never seen Griff treat any woman with anything other than respect, most times looking uncomfortable he thought smiling to himself . "I will contact him immediately and get him on board."

Del relaxed a little. His opinion of both Jennifer and Kevin went up with every meeting. They both stayed within their roles and made solid contributions. Kevin was a bear defending cubs with the finances. But he didn't use that stick to try and increase his influence on the Committee. In some ways it was dangerous to change something that was working so efficiently. However, the need for military involvement was real and it neatly solved the problem of having to deal with Griff's suspicions. Wasn't the first time a member of the Guard had gone missing. It will be quite a shock for Griff to learn the answer is space-based slavers. He's not going to like that answer. But once he gets the whole picture he'll understand why our hands are tied.

As Del left the chamber he mused over how much to tell Griff. On the one hand the BIG secret was instrumental in Pacifica's range of possible actions. On the other hand, protecting its secrecy was life or death for all of Pacifica. He would have to figure out a way to prepare Griff for all the possible alternatives while still keeping much from him. Griff was smart and much more intuitive than most gave him credit for. It was easy to think of him as a knuckle dragger. But that couldn't be further from the truth. Del had been verbally sparing with Griff for two decades and enjoyed every minute of it. Thinking about their many tavern discussions, Del smiled to himself then grew reflective. The old world of Pacifica was nearing its end. Huge changes were in store for everyone. These changes would happen within his lifetime. As Del reflected on what had been a wonderful life, he prayed for his people's survival.

# CHAPTER 4

# KING KENNETH

It was much too early in the morning for an audience. But the Governor's First Minister had insisted. It was infuriating that he had to obey orders from a mere bureaucrat. He was the king of Liberty! It was especially aggravating given the youth of the First Minister.

Kenneth had been crowned a year and a half earlier on the death of his father. He was in his early forties with no remarkable attributes other than showing the effects of a gluttonous life. He was pudgy with light hair and pale skin that looked as if it had rarely seen the sun. He spent his days and evenings scheming to solidify his control over Liberty and his nights engaged in his 'hobby'. Kenneth thought his younger brothers' objections to his 'hobby' exposed a character weakness. However, his bleeding-hearted brother's objections to changes proposed for the constitution was what caused the current crisis. He was the king and should be able to do anything he desired. The concept of personal rights taking precedence over royal desires infuriated him.

The Governor's First Minister was a tall handsome dark-haired man with pale skin and penetrating eyes. He seemed young for such an exalted position. He wore simple but formal clothing tastefully adorned with understated but expensive jewelry. He casually wore an antique 20th century Patek Phillippe watch that screamed wealth and influence. His eyes bored into Kenneth demanding submission.

"We've backed you in your efforts to change the constitution and defeat your brothers' armies. Once you've eliminated him we expect you to quickly deliver on your

23

promises," the First Minister said sternly.

When his brother had staged a popular revolt Kenneth had turned to the Commonwealth for financial help. They were reminding him of his contractual promises. He needed to figure out how to slow that down or he would risk alienating support from the wealthy landowners and privately owned monopolies.

"I will deliver the imports and exports as promised but need time to institute the changes we discussed," Kenneth said.

"It's pretty simple. You enslave the peasants living in areas that supported the revolution. Put them to work mining natural resources and producing exportable products. Drop all tariffs on imports. This combination will increase taxes on Liberty's trade to the levels agreed upon," the emissary patiently but firmly explained.

Kenneth knew this was true. It also increased the wealthy landowner's income but not as much as they expected. It was going to be tricky keeping their support once they figured out that the bulk of the change in wealth distribution was going to Commonwealth taxes and his personal coffers. The effect of dropping import tariffs on local monopolies would be a disaster inviting dissent. However, with the landowner's support and control of the military he could weather that storm.

He had panicked when his brother organized a popular revolt. That he had done so because of the proposed changes to the constitution surprised him. Why worry about a bunch of peasants? He initially assumed General Eastbrook would back his brother. They were friends after all. That meant he would need an influx of Commonwealth credits to secure mercenaries if he hoped to survive. To his utter shock and surprise, he had retained General Eastbrook's support. Eastbrook's support meant the bulk of the military stayed loyal. The General had remained to protect his "rightful king." What a joke that was. In Kenneths' opinion whoever held power was king. It was as simple as that.

The generals misplaced loyalty to the oaths sworn to his father was irrational. It was definitely something to be used to Kenneths' advantage. When he was a teenager his father had become concerned about Kenneths' fitness to be king. He had discovered Kenneths' 'hobby' and gotten a behavioral scientist from the university to do an analysis. The university woman who spent a great deal of time talking with him eventually told his father he lacked empathy. She even went as far as to tell the king his eldest son was best described as a psychopath. His father, being the sap that he was, decided Kenneth just needed love and understanding. It was just a phase. It was pretty easy to manipulate his father once he learned what a psychopath was and how to emulate and use empathy to his advantage. Unfortunately, his younger brother never bought the act.

"Well, my brother hasn't been defeated yet. Let's discuss details once that's done," Kenneth said attempting a delaying tactic to end the audience.

"The Governor has done her part in securing the loan. Now it's time for you to do your part. She is starting to believe you're intentionally delaying. If delays continue it won't be hard to convince a Commonwealth judge that you've violated your contract and issue an avoidance of taxes decision," the First Minister said with a knowing smile. "As you know the Governor has a reputation for being quite aggressive in these cases. My personal belief is that she enjoys meriting out justice."

Kenneth's stomach clenched and a cold sweat greased his palms. The facade dropped for a moment, and he said nervously, "this will be over quickly. Taxes will be generated. You have my word."

"I don't want your word. I want you to do what you promised and do it quickly," the First Minister said coldly. Then he insultingly turned and left without saying another word.

Kenneth sat for a few minutes trying to figure out a way to escape the trap he was in. Realizing he was out of options he decided he needed to take a walk and plan what to do. The delays were at an end and an aggressive plan needed to be executed quickly.

General William (Perry) Eastbrook was irritated but you wouldn't know it by looking at him. He appeared to be relaxed and sitting patiently waiting for his audience with the king. The king was late, and punctuality was somewhat of an obsession for Perry. His subordinates learned this quickly and joked quietly about it behind his back. Perry was of average height, slender yet muscular. He had olive skin and a hawkish face. He took great care with his physical conditioning and personal appearance. As the fourth son of a poor farmer his only opportunity in life was to join the military and hope for the best. A combination of intelligence, luck, hard work, and battlefield success had culminated in his appointment as General of the Royal Armed Forces. More than anyone else he was responsible for Liberty being under one government. After decades of perpetual war, he succeeded in conquering the despotic kingdoms that had opposed his king. He had united the planet. He could have declared himself king at that point. He was wildly popular not only with his compatriots but also with the populations that had been suffering under oppressive governments. A student of history, he emulated Alexander the Greats habit of recruiting his defeated enemies instead of punishing or imprisoning them. He had been successful in wooing them into his fold by treating them more honorably than their former kingdoms had. His answer to calls for him to take the crown was, "I am a simple soldier and have sworn an oath to my rightful king."

Everyone called him Perry. It was short for 'The Peregrine.' Prince Justin, the king's younger brother, had named him this after Perry saved the young, confused, and scared prince's first command from disaster. Prince Justin was an avid falconer and said the soldier reminded him of the lightning quick vicious strikes of a peregrine falcon. Perry had taken charge of the unit in the midst of chaos. He did this without having been given the authority to do so. He opened up a retreat path with a series of precise attacks against weak points in the encircling armies' lines. Many of royal blood would have been insulted. Many would have denied they had needed a common born soldier to extricate them from their mistakes. Prince Justin was an honorable man and gave Perry his well-deserved accolades. He then became his sponsor and vocal supporter helping to move him up the ranks. The name stuck much to his embarrassment.

The royal receptionist came over politely and said, "the king will see you now General Eastbrook."

Perry handed his weapons over to the two guards standing to either side of an impressive set of double doors. He walked in and nodded briefly to the four guards inside the reception room. Two were just inside of the doors and two were situated to either side of the king. They were six of his best. He hated seeing them used as guards. But given his personal opinion of the king he needed to have eyes and ears close by. They must be dying from boredom he thought. Perry saluted and then stood with his hands clasped behind his back and said, "you requested my presence Your Majesty."

"It's time Perry. Storm the castle and end this thing," the king said forcefully.

What's changed thought Perry. He could have ended this months ago. It was getting harder and harder to explain to his troops why they were just sitting around. Not that he minded giving Prince Justin more time. It bothered him deeply to be pressed into this duty, but duty it was. The prince was a longtime sponsor, friend, and a good man. But oaths took precedence over friendship. Oaths also took precedence over his conviction that the prince would make a much better king than this one.

"If we can promise safe exile for the families of the rebels I believe I can end this without bloodshed," Perry responded.

"Why should I care about the families of those who have forsaken their rightful king," Kenneth answered with a sneer.

"Because a castle siege, even a quick one, is a bloody affair and we need those troops to defend against Arista should they decide we are ripe for invasion," Perry responded. He had thought about his answer to this ever since they surrounded the castle. He knew the king would not be swayed by non-combatant arguments, even children. It had to be something that benefited him.

Kenneth hesitated to think it over then said, "give my brother assurances the rebel families will be spared if they surrender without delay. The families will be exiled to safe locations."

"I will execute that immediately Your Majesty," Perry said. He saluted and backed out of the room.

Instead of leaving the royal apartments he turned into the corridor leading to the Crown Princess's suite. He nodded at the salutes of the guards stationed outside her door and the second set of guards located just inside before he heard. "Dad, I didn't know you were coming." A beautiful young woman ran up and leapt into his arms embracing him tightly. A single tear ran down her face which she quickly wiped away smiling broadly.

"It was a last-minute summons by the king. Sorry Bria but a note wouldn't have beaten me here," Perry said smiling as another young woman looking remarkably like Bria walked up.

"Your Highness," Perry said as he bowed and then straightening up he grinned.

"Oh stop, Uncle Perry," she said with an affected grimace that couldn't keep from turning into a smile. "I know you have to do that in public but not here," she admonished him. Olivia had known Bria and her father as long as she could remember. When she was a toddler she had heard the guards refer to him as Perry and believed he was one of her uncles. As a toddler she had called him Uncle Perry in front of the entire royal court to uproarious laughter. It became an endearment.

"You both look wonderful, a sight for sore eyes." Perry shook his head and remarked, "the two of you look like twins. Are you ever going to stop copying each other?"

"No," they both said simultaneously and then looked at each other and broke into giggles.

They were of a similar height, slender with pale skin, blue eyes, and black hair pulled on top of their heads. Even the combs holding their hair up matched. If you looked closely Olivia had a softer slightly less athletic look about her. But they definitely looked like siblings. Those who didn't know them often confused them to their delight. Although their physical appearance was uncannily similar their personalities were not. Princess Olivia was a queen in the making. Intelligent, decisive, outspoken, and tough minded when needed. Bria was also intelligent but quiet, introspective, and soft spoken. They both agreed that Bria was actually the more stubborn of the two.

"Are you planning the wedding?" Perry asked.

This elicited frowns from both of them with Olivia saying, "yes, but I'm not happy about it. Lord Druango is twice my age, fat, grumpy, with no sense of humor. He's a cruel man. I know I have to marry to solidify the crown, but couldn't he have found someone a bit more suitable?"

"I'm sure he did the best he could Olivia," Perry said.

"Uncle Perry, please don't mouth politically appropriate nonsense to me. He could not care less for my well-being, and you know it," Olivia said bluntly.

Lord Druango was extremely rich and the power behind the previous Kingdom of Druango. The actual king of Druango had been a pawn. He had been assassinated by 'unknown assailants' in the final days before Perry had marched into their capital city. It was well known who ordered his assassination but without evidence there was little that could be done.

The engagement was a good move politically, and financially, but at what cost? Perry knew part of the reason Olivia and Bria copied each other was their fantasy of being sisters. The fantasy included having him as their father. It was humbling to say the least. It added an extra layer of loyalty and commitment even beyond his unbreakable oath. She was the eventual queen of Liberty. "He's your father and you need to respect him. I'm sorry you have to do this for the crown. You know Bria and I will always be here for you."

This last promise was politically important. Lord Druango would try and take control when the current king died. Perry was the one man who could stop that and maintain Olivia's authority over the realm.

Olivia's mother had died under suspicious circumstances. Getting no love or support from her father, she begged him to go live with Uncle Perry and Bria. His reaction was to order the pre-teenage Bria to move into the Royal Castle as a companion for Olivia. The one concession Perry had gotten in return was to have them both at his ranch during the summers. This eliminated time the king was expected to spend with his daughter and provided a hostage against the good behavior of General Eastbrook when the House of Lords was in session. A win-win in his mind.

"Let's be honest with each other no matter what," Olivia said with warmth in her eyes. She then turned serious and asked, "will the siege be over soon?"

"That's why I'm here. I'm going to go and attempt to negotiate a surrender with your uncle. If that's not possible I'll have to take his castle," Perry said.

"Is there any way to save Uncle Justin?" Olivia said in a pleading voice.

"I'm sorry but there isn't. He rebelled against the rightful ruler of Liberty and his fate is sealed. Your aunt and cousins will be saved if he agrees to surrender. You know your uncle; he will sacrifice himself to protect them and prevent unnecessary bloodshed. He's a good man but there isn't anything that can be done."

They spent the next few hours discussing family, friends, and the wedding plans. Bria would be Olivia's maid of honor and had agreed to be her official companion until Bria married. While more than a little jealous, Olivia was pleased that Bria could marry whomever she wanted. She knew her Uncle Perry could gain monetary benefits from an arranged marriage but insisted his daughter's happiness came first. Olivia was dwelling on this when Perry said, "I'm sorry but I'd be derelict if I didn't leave now. The king insisted I get a surrender negotiated as soon as possible. Have loved seeing you both and will see you again as soon as this is over."

"Please tell Uncle Justin that I love him," Olivia said in a sad voice. Perry frowned but nodded his agreement.

Both young women hugged him fiercely and with their eyes shining Perry said his goodbyes, turned, and left.

As he left the Royal Castle Perry mused on the possible reasons for the abrupt change. He was missing something. He wondered if it had anything to do with the Commonwealth dandy he saw in the hallway that morning. It would not be surprising if the Commonwealth were playing politics with the king. Their only objective was higher taxes and Perry worried about what agreements might have been made. If there was one thing Perry was good at, it was compartmentalizing problems until something could be done about them. He decided to quit worrying about this sudden change and rode off towards Prince Justin's castle.

# CHAPTER 5

# OATH GIVER

Griff strolled into Del's office and plopped down in one of the chairs facing his desk. The man swaggers everywhere he goes thought Del. If anything, the stern expression he wore the last time he had seen him had intensified. Griff glared at Del and said, "since you asked me to come see you I assume you have something to tell me."

Del swallowed the smart-ass response normal for their interactions and said, "it's conditional. I have some things to discuss but only if you agree to join a group simply known as the Committee. Once you join you can't leave, it's a lifetime commitment."

"What kind of nonsense is this. I want to know what's going on with Tee and I expect you to tell me," Griff said forcefully leaning forward in a threatening way.

"You're not going to learn anything unless you agree. This is for the good of Pacifica. No amount of bullying is going to get me to open up. I promise you'll agree with the necessity for secrecy once you understand what we're doing. To do that you must join and agree to follow all rules and restrictions," Del said equally forcefully.

"What are the rules and restrictions?" Griff asked.

"I won't tell you anything until you agree to join and pledge an oath to comply. The rules and restrictions pertain to information that can't be divulged to anyone not a member of the Committee," Del said.

Griff just looked at him for a while clearly mulling it over. Then his frown deepened, and he said, "so I have to give you my oath to keep something secret for the rest of my life without knowing anything about it beforehand."

"Yes," Del answered.

"If I join the Committee and swear an oath will you tell me what happened to Tee?" Griff said with eyes boring into Del's.

"Yes," Del answered quickly. Then a moment later he said, "and I should not have told you that."

Griff took a deep breath, grimaced, and said, "if I didn't know you as well as I do, I would never agree to these ridiculous conditions. This had better be good or you and I are going to have a problem."

Del smiled for the first time and said, "I think you'll be satisfied with the reasons behind the need for secrecy. Do I have your agreement to join and your oath to abide by the rules and restrictions?"

Griff's frown disappeared, he visibly relaxed clearly accepting the situation. He took a deep breath, held up his hand mockingly and said, "I swear to join the Committee and abide by its rules and restrictions. Now what the hell is going on."

Del stood up and walked to his office door. He locked it. Turning back around he walked to a large wooden filing cabinet built into the wall. Unlocking and opening one of the bottom drawers, he reached in and fiddled with something until Griff heard a loud click. Del then rotated the entire cabinet away from the wall revealing a hidden stairway. He lit a lamp and beckoned Griff with a wave of his hand disappearing down the stairs into the dark.

"Pull that closed on your way down," Del called out.

Griff stepped through the doorway and closed the hidden door. A loud click let him know it was latched. He caught up with Del in a narrow hallway at the base of the stairs. "Where are we going?" he asked.

"Afraid of the dark?" Del responded attempting to revive

their usual banter.

"No," Griff replied. "If I'm going to murder someone I prefer to do it in the dark."

Del smiled, glad to hear his old friend sound like himself again. "We're headed to a secret complex of tunnels below the caves that everyone knows about. I'll explain more once we enter. While we are unlikely to be overheard down here we take extreme precautions outside of that space."

They followed a downward sloping tunnel which had a half dozen side tunnels randomly feeding into it. After a 5 minute walk the tunnel ended at a metal door that looked like the opening to a bank vault. Del took out a large key and opened the door which swung out and away from the opening. Ten feet away was an identical door. After they stepped through Del closed and locked the door behind him. Then he said, "when I open the next door you're going to see things you'll have a hard time believing. Once we lock that one behind us I'll start answering your questions."

Del opened the second door, and the small metal room was filled with light. Griff could hear a low humming noise and feel warm air filtering in through the doorway. Stepping out into the room Griff looked around in speechless wonder. The illumination was from some source other than open flame and was quite bright, daylight bright. Devices that looked like the computers in the ancient children's books were glowing and had pictures and images on them. Del caught the attention of a young man who was seated at one of these stations. Griff recognized him as the kid who got punched on the Apple Valley school playground.

"Quinn, this is Griff. He's a new member of the Committee. If he has questions for you in the future you are free to answer them just like you would any other Committee member," Del said.

Turning back to Griff he added, "Quinn is one of five engineering specialist's privy to much of what I'm going to tell you. You'll want to spend some time with him after we're done."

"You're the Guard member who invited Tee to recruit training," Quinn said smiling broadly.

"Do you know what happened to him?" Griff asked sternly.

Del held up his hands and said. "Patience Griff, there is a lot of background information you need before you can understand the situation. The short summary is that Tee is alive, unharmed, and relatively safe. He is a prisoner and unfortunately we don't have a way to rescue him. Come into the conference room and let me sketch out what's going on."

When they sat down Griff said accusingly, "we clearly didn't lose our technology."

"Not all of it, no. But before you ask why we aren't using it against the GEMs you need to hear the whole story. The short answer is that if we reveal our technology we all die." Del went on to explain how they had accidentally learned of the Commonwealth and the dangers of revealing themselves. Griff was shocked and a bit shaken to learn Pacifica natives were actually GEMs themselves. That he was a GEM. When Del got to the part where the Committee might decide that everyone had to commit suicide he just nodded his agreement. That's when Del knew Griff really understood the dire situation they were in. Once again he was impressed with Griff. The man had absorbed the shocking news much faster than Del had those many years ago. Del went on to explain how Pacifica's ability to delay interacting with the Commonwealth was coming to a close.

"So, we need a plan to roll out second generation warfare. That's the purpose of my being added to the Committee," Griff said.

Del gave a sigh and said, "it goes way beyond that Griff. We need more diversity on the Committee. We obviously have to keep the number of members to a minimum but in doing so we have the risk of limited perspective. We are likely to miss something important when making decisions.

You will be expected to weigh in on every issue that comes up. You were selected because of your intelligence, leadership, creativity, and ability to work in a team. It's not just because you are a professional soldier."

Griff considered this and then changing the subject asked, "so what happened to Tee?"

"Arista kidnapped him for their gladiatorial games. He's a slave. Based on intercepted communications we believe a sizable bribe was used to get approval from the Commonwealth to do this. Our civilization is designated as a primitive culture. We're supposed to be left alone. We don't understand if this was even legal by Commonwealth law. The best case is that Pacifica gets accepted as a colony and we successfully challenge the legality of Tee's slave status. Unfortunately, because of the dangers involved neither of us will be around to celebrate," Del said.

"So, we'll never see him again," Griff said.

"Unlikely either of us will. It's possible his family could get him back at some point," Del said. "The reason Pacifica is out of options is that the GEMs have run out of room. Their high reproduction rate has outstripped their food production. They are highly motivated to expand into the peninsula. The crisis is causing them to cooperate which is why so many more GEMs were involved in the latest attack. The opinion of the Commonwealth survey ship orbiting Pacifica is that they will overwhelm our defenses sometime in the next two years. You know better than I how close we came to losing the Wall this last time. Once the Wall is breached it won't take long until the Landfall Dam is threatened. The Committee has always thought that is when we pull out second-generation weapons to defend ourselves. Now that you are on the Committee we'll look to you for advice on timing and execution. Once we use that technology the Commonwealth will take over. The good news is they will eliminate the GEMs. The bad news is that if we aren't incredibly lucky everyone on Pacifica will be enslaved or killed. Pacifica has an abundance of natural resources. The

Commonwealth wants to legally convert us from being designated as a primitive culture to a Commonwealth colony. Since we are adapted to heavy planet activities there is motivation to enslave rather than kill. There is also speculation of turning the Guard into slave mercenaries. Turns out they believe we have the most effective warriors in the Commonwealth."

Griff considered this for a while, then he asked, "what technologies do we have access to?"

Del nodded his head, grinned, and then said. "We have the entire set of logs and libraries from the colony ships. It is a tremendous resource of technical information and know-how. We believe some of what we have is now banned technology. Even Commonwealth citizens don't have access to it. What we don't have is most of the technology itself. This set of rooms is contained in a structure called a faraday cage. It keeps all electrical signals from detection by the Commonwealth. The electronic equipment we have consists of a variety of radios and computer systems. This was put together just before the Colony war. Obviously, we were suspicious of the GEMs intentions before they attacked. We stockpiled backup systems, spare parts, and even printed service manuals for critical systems. Below us is an underground river we use to drive an electric generator that runs what you saw in the other room. We also have a fully provisioned computer operated machine shop to service and repair critical elements. We can make damn near anything with that equipment. All of these areas are shielded."

"Ok, what weapons do I have access to? "Griff asked.

"There is a planetary defense system in mothballs. But there is no way we could install and activate it. Even if we could, these systems were designed to be used in concert with space-based warships. The Commonwealth knows how to defeat these types of defensive systems so trying to employ one would just be a form of delayed suicide. There are two space shuttles in storage as well. As far as we can tell they both work. At least they pass their diagnostics. But until we try and use them who knows. We can't use any high-level technology because the Commonwealth will see that as tax evasion. Our designation as a primitive culture is basically a tax exemption for the sector. It is illegal to hide technological sophistication in an attempt to stay in a primitive state under their Edicts. It's even worse if we are discovered to have second-generation or later weapons of any kind. In that case the Commonwealth would consider us to be in rebellion. Either of these situations would authorize sector government to assume control of the planet and enslave or kill the population. So, we have to 'invent' second-generation weapons in a way that is believable. And we have to destroy everything else," Del said.

"You've obviously thought about all of this so where do I start?" Griff asked.

"Black powder. We have all the raw materials and the formula for making it. Producing guns would make it obvious have been hiding technological advances. Some sort of weapon that drops bombs in front of the Wall is an idea. Burying bombs in the sand and detonating them from the Wall is another," Del said.

"How are we going to explain black powder suddenly showing up?" Griff asked.

"A little luck has helped us there. A farmer discovered black powder by accident a decade ago. He developed it to the point where he was entertaining his family and neighbors with crude explosions. The Committee decided to buy his silence and move the discovery to the university. We intercepted communications indicating the Commonwealth detected the gunpowder. They decided that since we haven't used it for anything other than entertainment we're still below the threshold for conversion to a colony. Our story is that we hid it because we were worried about public safety. When the GEMs looked like they would overwhelm us we realized it could be used as a weapon," Del said.

Griff nodded his head thoughtfully and said, "how do we test our ideas without the Commonwealth sensing the explosions?"

"It doesn't have to work all that well. The intent is enough. Our goal is to demonstrate second-generation weapons capabilities. Once we do that the Commonwealth will take over. We have an extensive library that includes detailed instructions for weapons manufacture from simple chemical weapons to fission, fusion, and anti-matter devices. Of course, we don't have the refined materials for the latter three so that information is rather useless. We are confident of building something that will work." Del paused, and then said, "you can ask Quinn questions, but I'll assign one of the other students to work with you on this. Keep in mind we're looking for ideas. We must save the people of Pacifica and perhaps there is another way."

Del got up and motioned Griff to follow him. "Let's take a break and go have a little fun."

"There isn't anything remotely fun about any of this," Griff said seriously.

Del just kept walking and turned down a corridor which ended with another locked door. He produced yet another key from his pocket, unlocked and opened the door. "This is our advanced weapons arsenal and lab," Del said as he swept his hand around the room.

Griff was dumbstruck trying to take it all in. Along the back wall of the room was a rack of approximately one hundred devices. They had stocks and triggers like a crossbow with two round tubes aligned with where an arrow would be placed on that device. The other end of the room was clearly a firing range with silhouette targets and of all things a pumpkin on a stand. Motioning over at the racks of devices Griff said, "what comes out of the tubes."

"The bottom tube is a battery. That's an energy storage device. The top is the discharge tube. By the way, part of our historical cleansing was to confiscate all the adult level books describing technology. We left the children's books so that it would be less shocking if and when we trotted all this out. It was a nice story that paper books were only printed for children." Del then picked up one of the devices and continued, "this was originally a bunker built in anticipation of the Colony war. It's the only thing that survived. These weapons were for defending the bunker. It's an energy weapon. Three settings. Safe, kill, and stun." He said as he pointed to a switch clearly marked with these designations. When kill is activated it will burn a hole completely through clothing and flesh but not metal. Evidently these models were for use aboard spacecraft. You can imagine the problems with weapons aboard a spacecraft. We have plans for altering these to basically burn through anything. Not currently a high priority for us." Del flipped the switch to kill, turned, aimed, and burned a hole right through the chest area on one of the cloth silhouette targets. Motioning Griff forward they inspected the cherry sized hole in the cloth and the slightly blemished metal plate behind it.

"Why don't you take a few shots." Del said grinning like a teenage boy.

Griff smiled and accepted the offer then blasted away for a while. At Del's suggestion he shot the pumpkin which not only drilled a hole but caused the pumpkin to emit smoke from the burning skin and pulp inside. Smiling broadly, he said. "That's incredible. And you're right it's fun." He thought about this for a few moments and started asking questions. "How many shots can it fire?"

Del nodded his head and said, "ninety to one hundred and then it needs to be recharged. The recharge currently takes almost a day. We have schematics for a fast charger. But it involves changes to our power grid that would be quite a bit of work. Another thing low on the priority list."

"How do you know how well it works on flesh," Griff asked with concern.

"We didn't use it on people if that's what you're asking," Del said with his face scrunched up in mock disgust. Smiling he then said, "we've taken haunches of beef and drilled holes through them. Doesn't seem to matter how thick the haunch is. The hole goes all the way through.

"Tell me about the stun setting," Griff asked.

"The stun setting was initially a little more challenging to test from an ethical standpoint. One of our university students long ago decided to volunteer. He reported that it was just like falling asleep. No pain, no apparent aftereffects at all. The literature on it says it immediately forces the brain into a delta wave pattern, or deep sleep. It maintains this pattern for one to three hours. The person doesn't feel pain and cannot be woken up. Dr. Espers is very enthusiastic about using it for general anesthesia. The brain eventually transitions through the normal brain wave functions you would expect on anyone going from deep sleep to wakefulness. The test subject said it just feels like a good nap," Del concluded.

"How accurately does it need to be aimed? How selective is it?" Griff asked.

"That turns out to be a complicated question and one we did extensive testing to figure out. Once we were certain there weren't negative side effects we gathered more volunteers. It seems to be a function of the field strength of the wave when it encounters the subject. Quinn can give you the details. To give you an idea, if the end of this room were filled with people one shot would put them all asleep. In the stun setting you only get twenty to twenty-five shots."

Griff grew serious at this point obviously thinking it all through. He then looked to have reached a decision and said forcefully, "I will honor my oath and comply with decisions made by the Committee. We share the same primary goal of protecting our people, but my objective is victory. I don't plan on losing to the Commonwealth."

Del just nodded his head showing his understanding but thought to himself that he had made the right choice. A few moments later he added, "you should have a high-level understanding of our technology knowledge base and sector history as we understand it. This is going to take some time to digest. I'll leave you with Quinn to start that process and see you at the next Committee meeting." As he walked away he thought, We have the same end goal old friend. I don't know how we pull off the herculean task of beating the Commonwealth. But it doesn't mean we shouldn't try. We will likely go down, but like you, I want to go down swinging.

# CHAPTER 6

# THE GOVERNOR

The First Minister was always nervous meeting with the Governor. It wasn't the power of her office that caused his anxiety. He was used to interacting with the great and powerful in the Commonwealth. He was one of them after all. It was the way she looked at him. She was cat-like. Her pitiless stare didn't give you any indication of whether she was preparing to pounce or would just swish her tail and walk away. Her unusual appearance made her behavior even more disturbing. She had stark white hair cut short with mismatched eyes. One blue and one green. She had a trim figure with perfect smooth bronze colored skin. Most people thought she was extremely attractive. These were people who didn't know her.

"Good afternoon Jack. I hope you have good news for me," Governor Jacobs said locking him with her cat eyes and sly smile.

"Good afternoon Governor. We have a commitment from King Kenneth to finish his brother off. However, he's still arguing to delay the changes needed to increase tax revenues. He's on notice that further delays will result in a request for a tax avoidance judgement," Jack said with his hands clenched tightly together behind his back.

The Governor just stared at him, not indicating pleasure or anger at his report. Finally, after an uncomfortable amount of time she said, "our goal is getting the legal authority in Liberty to change the constitution. Punishment of the rebels will allow him to get 'emergency changes' through a diminished House of Lords. Once fully implemented we can move forward with the proposal from Magistrate Pluta. Anything that stops constitutional change destroys the plan. I hope you have everything in place to insure nothing unfortunate happens."

Jack had to collect himself before answering. He was very good at keeping emotions off his face. But he felt she could see right through that and was enjoying his discomfort. "The key Lords have signed taxation contracts in exchange for their votes. As promised they have used their advances to fund mercenaries who are ready for the final military phase."

"Will the mercenaries be able to force a quick marriage so that Lord Druango can eventually take control of the planet?" she asked.

"That's the plan. King Kenneth has no ethics, morals, or loyalties. He is a psychopath and megalomaniac who lacks good judgement. His ego is so out of control that he doesn't see the threat in Lord Druango. If nothing else, this is proof we can't depend on him. We can't even depend on him to make the right decisions in his own self-interest. Druango promises King Kenneth will have an accident soon after the wedding," Jack said.

"Any indications that Druango is going to change his mind with respect to the slave trade?" she asked.

"He has remained consistent with what he wants. I think we can count on him as long as he gets his cut of the revenues as proposed by Magistrate Pluta."

The Governor nodded her head accepting his explanation and then said, "does our friend in Arista have control of the emperor?"

"He says he does but I have reason to doubt that. While Pluta is the current magistrate for the senate there is a younger aggressive senator who appears to be chipping away at his influence. They are both entirely motivated by money. We can probably come to an agreement with either one," Jack said.

"Have you spoken with this young senator?" The

Governor asked her eyes narrowing.

"I met Senator Cereo at a party he held in his Roma domus just last month," Jack said. "He's very charismatic. He's clearly the leader of the 'new money' senators and is slowly expanding his influence with 'old money' votes."

"That's unusual isn't it? I thought Arista was quite stogy in their belief of old order superiority," she said with an expression on her face that indicated she didn't believe him.

"I learned at the party that he's descended from one of the original senatorial families. He's actually distantly related to the emperor. His parents squandered the family fortune and went bankrupt. He started with nothing and is now the richest man in Arista. Or soon will be. He does get insulted in private for 'dirtying his hands' by the old order senators but it's more a respectful jibe. He is highly respected for turning around his families' fortunes. The old order see him as proving their theory of superiority while the 'new money' senators believe he is one of their own, having come up the hard way," Jack said.

"Young and aggressive sounds better than old and stogy. Why don't we prefer to work with him?" the Governor asked.

"The difficulty is we can't predict who the emperor will listen to. As you know all real power in Arista rests in the emperors' hands. The senate's authority stops at managing the planet. They can propose actions and decrees, but the emperor must approve them. They can't negotiate treaties or declare war. The current emperor is gluttonous, lazy, and prone to making arbitrary decisions. He's too entitled for us to work directly with him. All he really cares about are blood sports and pleasure slaves. Both senators keep their own stable of gladiators because it gives them audience time with the emperor," Jack explained.

"While we're on that subject, were our friends successful in capturing one of those Pacifica brutes for the magistrate?" the Governor asked.

"Yes they did. As you know Pacifica is extremely remote. It will take time to execute the large number of jumps to get back to Arista," Jack replied. He thought for a moment and then said, "You might get a complaint from Sector Judicial. The Chief Justice was not comfortable approving this even after the outrageous bribe. Their hands have been well greased, so no one should have anything to complain about. Their excuse of indigenous research is inspired but weak. Given similar cases I'm familiar with they will merely get their hands slapped if they get caught," Jack said.

"Sector Judicial are a bunch of whiny assholes. It's no surprise they take the credits and then complain," the Governor said with distain. "So, Magistrate Pluta's excuse for requesting the kidnapping was access to the emperor?"

"Yes, but I'm pretty sure it wasn't the only reason. The senator also enjoys his blood sports a little too much," Jack said.

"You don't approve?" she said narrowing her eyes and examining him.

"I don't approve of anyone we are depending on having distractions," Jack said.

The governor considered his answer then slowly nodded her head and asked, "any other weaknesses to exploit?"

"He enjoys driving aristocrats who don't work hard or fall on back luck into bankruptcy. Appears to be a hobby of sorts. If having a significant number of impoverished formerly wealthy individuals hating your guts is a weakness, then we can put it on the list," Jack explained.

"At least he's shown himself to be a clever negotiator. Let's make sure he doesn't get too clever," the Governor said with an amused smile. "Keep me updated on Liberty and Arista."

"Yes ma'am," Jack said then turned and walked out of her office relieved for the audience to be over. He had been unsettled with the plan from the beginning. Jack liked plans to be simple. In his opinion a good plan relied on as few people as possible. All with a history of being predictable. Jack would be losing sleep until large shipments of slaves were actually leaving Liberty.

CHAPTER 7

# SURRENDER

Why did he have to smile thought Perry. The prince greeted him warmly, treating him as an honored guest and friend. Perry already felt terrible about doing this. An angry accusatory posture would be much more appropriate and easier to handle.

"You look well Perry," the prince said. "Although that frown you're wearing doesn't go well with your face."

"This isn't pleasant and you're making it harder than it already is," Perry responded with a hint of anger.

"Let's enjoy each other's company one more time my friend. We both know this will be over soon," the prince said with a sad smile. "Tell me how Bria is doing." He said this with his trademark devilish smile brightening a bit.

Perry remembered once again why he liked and admired this man. No matter the circumstances, no matter the station of the person, he was almost always gracious and thoughtful. So different than his brother. The Prince did have a temper. He could be a devil when he thought someone was being unfair or treating others badly. They had argued when the prince had proposed deposing the king. He vividly remembered the conversation.

"My brother has a serious mental illness Perry. He's unfit to rule. My father was deceived as to his true nature, or he would have passed over him," the prince had said.

"I swore an oath to support the succession and be loyal to the king in all regards," Perry said. "I cannot support you becoming king."

"I'm not asking you to make me king. My niece is not her father. Bria is Olivia's best friend for heaven's sake. You know her better than I do. You know she would be an excellent ruler."

"I've sworn an oath," was all Perry would say further on the matter.

Back in the present Perry hesitated a bit and then said in a business-like tone, "both Bria and Olivia are fine. Olivia told me to tell you she loves you. They are both worried about you but mature enough to understand the situation. I'm here with an offer. You surrender and the families will be spared. They will be separated and exiled to locations that will be determined later. They will be safe, and they won't be impoverished."

"Did my brother promise this?" the prince responded.

"Yes," said Perry.

"This is obviously your idea. You know his word is meaningless."

"I will die to protect the families. You have my word," Perry said.

"Now that is something I can count on," the prince said in a serious tone. "Give us this evening to spend with our families and I'll surrender at noon tomorrow. I do this based on your personal honor and nothing else Perry."

Perry always woke two hours before dawn. This was his time to attack thorny problems, work on battle strategies, time to think without interruption. It was the best time of his day. This morning was not pleasant. Going through the motions of surrender would be easy enough. But putting the prince and old friends in chains was going to test his resolve. Many of the rebellious officers were previously trusted advisors to whom he owed a large debt of gratitude.

But what was on his mind this morning was Lord Barrows. The Lord had shown up the day before with a sealed order authorizing him to accept the surrender on the king's behalf. That didn't set off alarms, but the special guard squad sent to escort him did. It wasn't a concern that the king's representative had a guard detail to protect him. It was that Perry didn't recognize any of the soldiers. Perry had a remarkable ability to remember names and faces. He had never seen any of these men before.

He called out, "corporal, go get Captain Peters for me."

"He's likely still asleep General," the corporal responded.

"Wake him up. I need him here as soon as he's presentable."

A few minutes later a young, groggy, and rumpled officer showed up, saluted, and said, "Peters, here as ordered sir."

Perry looked him over nodding his head in approval at Peters decision to forgo appearance for speed and said, "Peters, I have a special assignment for you this morning."

Perry walked out of his tent 10 minutes before the surrender was scheduled to begin. He would be 5 minutes early per his long-maintained habit of punctuality. As he walked out Captain Peters and four burly veteran soldiers formed up in a protective diamond formation around him. Anyone in the Royal Armed Forces seeing this would be surprised since Perry never used bodyguards. His sword and knives were not decorative. As they walked towards the castle gates Perry asked Captain Peters in a low voice, "is everything in place?"

"Yes sir," he replied.

Perry grunted an acknowledgement but said no more.

A large tent had been erected just in front of the castle gates to hold the formal surrender proceedings. The formal declaration of surrender had been sent the previous evening for the prince's review. This wasn't a negotiation; it was a courteous gesture by Perry so Prince Justin would know beforehand what was required of him.

Lord Barrows was incensed the previous evening when he

found out. He had barged into Perry's command tent interrupting a staff discussion and declared, "you have no authority to write or deliver the surrender contract. That duty was given to me by the king."

Perry calmly continued the discussion he was having with one of his staff members ignoring him. When the conversation ended he slowly turned and stared at Lord Barrows until Lord Barrows looked away. Then Perry said, "this is a military operation. Until the surrender is formally accepted I am in charge. I have always written and delivered surrender agreements. In the past I also accepted surrenders on behalf of the king. The king's orders stated you were to accept surrender on his behalf. Nothing else."

"I don't agree with the terms of surrender you offered that traitor," Lord Barrows said looking down his nose at Perry.

"The king gave me the terms of surrender personally and asked me to negotiate on his behalf. You have no authority to change my previous orders. I was directed to complete this surrender as soon as possible and that is what I'm going to do," Perry said firmly.

"You will answer to the king for this," Lord Barrows shouted as he turned around and walked out.

"As will you Lord Barrows," Perry said quietly as the tent flaps swung back in place.

One of strengths of Perry's army was its surveillance capabilities. He had agents embedded everywhere. Perry had recognized the value of surveillance early in the Unification Wars. The competing kingdoms were both corrupt. That made it easy to bribe or pay retainers for information. He learned that you never knew where key strategic information would come from. The more informants the better. Of course, this meant he had more opportunities for double agents. But as long as you treated all of them as double agents', useful information could be deciphered and corroborated.

Lord Barrows had one of Perry's agents on his personal staff. He had copied the Lord's surrender document and passed it over. The terms of surrender were quite different from what had been sent to Prince Justin. It was cleverly worded. Without time to work through the language at the surrender table Prince Justin could easily have misunderstood the agreement to be promising safety for the families of the rebels. In reality it was an unconditional surrender with no concrete promises. This was contrary to what Perry had negotiated and he would not allow it.

Perry and Lord Barrows stood next to the open-air tent as the castle gate opened and Prince Justin with two retainers walked out. Perry was the first to greet them, "good morning Your Highness."

To which Lord Barrows said forcefully, "he's not a prince anymore, the king removed his title."

Prince Justin ignored this and said, "good morning General Eastbrook, Lord Barrows."

He's a better man than I am thought Perry. Even in these circumstances he maintains perfect decorum. Perry then said, "let's review the terms and process steps of surrender and I'll answer any questions you have."

"Thank you General Eastbrook for sending the surrender document last night. It matches our discussion, and I have no questions." With that Prince Justin motioned one of his retainers to hand over the document sent the previous evening. He took a deep breath and signed it with a flourish. His whole body visibly relaxed at that point seemingly accepting his fate. Prince Justin then motioned to his other retainer who made a hand signal back to the castle.

The main gate opened, and the rebels streamed out of the castle in a single file. The officers came last. Most were familiar to Perry as he had fought alongside them in many battles. A few brought a grim painful smile to his face. They handed in their weapons at a table set up for this purpose and then walked to another table for processing. Political leaders and officers were separated as they would be put on trial. They expected to be hung but accepted this fate as payment for their family's safety. Everyone else was to be let go after swearing allegiance to the king.

When the stream of rebels stopped coming from the castle Perry sent in a squad to search for anyone hidden away. After a few hours it was declared to be populated entirely by non-combatants. This was a testament to the trust the rebels had in Prince Justin.

Perry turned to Lord Barrows and said, "I'm satisfied that all terms of surrender have been met. You can sign for the king now."

Lord Barrows smiled and turning to Prince Justin he said, "the surrender contract you signed is null and void. I require your signature on the official one authorized by the king."

Perry said, "this is not my understanding based on discussions with the king. I will not support this."

Lord Barrows smiled even wider turning to his captain of the guard and said, "arrest General Eastbrook. He is charged with treason and will be delivered to the king for judgement along with the others."

Upon that pronouncement one of the servants attending them drove a large knife into Lord Barrows Captain of the Guard. The rest of Lord Barrows men within the surrender tent were quickly overwhelmed by more of Peters men who were also donning servant's garb. The mercenaries outside the tent were quickly cut down in a barrage of arrows.

Lord Barrow was in shock. "You can't do this. I have the authority of the king."

Perry looked at him confidently and said, "At this point you have no authority. You're going to tell me exactly what the king told you to do."

Although full of bluster, Lord Barrows wasn't dedicated to anything other than himself. It didn't take much persuasion for self-preservation to take over. He spilled his guts while begging for mercy. The most immediate problem was an army of mercenaries on its way to take over operations. They had orders to slaughter the rebels and their families. Even the children. They were primarily off-world mercenaries with a few from Druango. That region had a longstanding reputation for brutality. The Lord of that region was Princess Olivia's fiancée. Now that Perry knew the plan it was a simple thing to occupy the castle and eliminate the threat.

Perry walked back to join Prince Justin, sat down, and signed the surrender document.

"What are you going to do?" Prince Justin asked, a smile now on his face.

"I'm going to go have a discussion with the king," Perry responded. Turning he beckoned his second in command over. "Colonel Fedral, you are in command. Prince Justin is under your protection and will comply with orders spelled out under the surrender agreement. You will occupy the castle and deny access to the mercenaries who will arrive shortly. This includes the authority to arm any rebels who swear to follow your orders, and you feel are necessary to execute those orders. If opportunity presents itself you can use your judgement and go on the offensive against the mercenaries. You are not to follow anyone's orders other than those I give you personally."

Colonel Fedral turned to Prince Justine and said, "Your Highness, will you assist me in moving everyone back into the castle?"

Prince Justin grinned broadly and said. "It would be a pleasure Colonel. I will publicly swear fealty to your authority and encourage everyone to do the same."

"Thank you Your Highness," Colonel Fedral said respectfully.

Perry turned to Captain Peters and said "Pull together one hundred of your best Rangers. We leave for the Royal Castle in 15 minutes."

# CHAPTER 8

# SUCCESSOR

Perry surprised the king's receptionist; walking in with no advance notice, covered in dust, with a severe look in his eyes.

"General Eastbrook, we didn't know you had returned from the siege," the receptionist said with panic showing on his face. It was obvious he never expected to see Perry again. "I don't have any openings for an audience today."

Perry ignored him and walked up to the surprised throne room guards and handed them his sword. They saluted and when he motioned them to open the doors they did.

The king was speechless as Perry walked purposefully towards him. Perry was supposed to be dead along with the king's brother and all of the rebels, including their families. Clearly Barrows had failed.

The king finally found his voice as Perry approached him. "Arrest General Eastbrook. He has committed treason against the crown."

"Stand down," Perry ordered forcefully without turning to face the Guards. They dutifully resumed their positions. These guards had been hand-picked by

Perry. They were from families owing allegiance to him. Families he knew to be completely loyal and trustworthy.

"What are you doing?" the king asked, fear clearly on his face.

"Something I should have done long ago," Perry said as he quickly drew a knife from his sleeve and drove it forcefully into King Kenneth's chest piecing his heart. He pulled the knife out, grabbed the king by the hair, pulled his head back, and slit his throat. His training as a Ranger taught him to double up on killing blows when it was critical for the enemy to stay down. It was always good to be thorough.

As the king lay with blood gurgling out onto the stone floor Perry said casually to the guards, "you can arrest me for treason now."

"Sir?" was the nervous response from the young man in charge. He was the youngest son of a close family friend. Perry had known him since he was a toddler. He hated putting the young man in this situation. The young soldier looked terrified at the prospect of arresting the godlike personage of General Eastbrook.

"Richard," he said kindly. "Go out in the hallway and find Captain Peters. Bring him here."

"Yes sir," Richard said saluting. He then hurried off out the door.

Perry shook his head slowly, his face relaxing into an amused grin. He guessed he ought to accept that as a compliment. It did bother him that he could walk into the throne room, assassinate the king, and then have his orders obeyed by guards sworn to protect the king with their lives. He guessed it had as much to do with the guard's distaste for the king as loyalty to him. They must have been privy to all kinds of disturbing knowledge, including questions about the rumors surrounding the king's 'hobby'."

"Sir," said Captain Peters a few moments later.

"The king is dead. I murdered him. Go secure the queen. Inform her of what has happened. Tell her my recommendation is to place you in charge of castle security until other arrangements can be made. Lock down the castle until you are assured of the queen's safety. You can trust the king's and queen's guards. They were hand-picked by me and will be loyal to the queen. Once she places them under your authority do what you think is best. Arrest me and have these guards place me in the dungeon for now," Perry said motioning to the king's guards still obviously in shock. "You have much to do Captain, better get going."

"Yes sir, thank you sir," Captain Peters said with gratitude in his eyes. Perry continued to be impressed with Peters. He had obviously figured out what Perry was going to do and had resolved to support it anyway. Peters was bright enough to realize that Perry had not filled him in on the plan to protect him from accusations of involvement in a treasonous conspiracy. All Peters had to do was tell the truth. He had simply been following reasonable orders.

Perry spent about two hours in the dungeon before the queen showed up with Captain Peters, the Chief Justice, and the Queen's Guard. "I want General Eastbrook moved to a more secure location until the trial," she said looking sternly at Perry.

She was a pretty good actress but couldn't hide the warmth in her eyes, Perry thought. Unfortunately, she would need to get much better at hiding her thoughts and emotions. His heart went out to her, she was much too young to be forced into this situation.

Turning around the queen said, "Captain Peters. There is an unused apartment at the top of the residence tower. The only access is through a narrow stairway located in an alcove at the west end of the third-floor hallway. Bar the doors at the top and bottom of the stairway. Place whatever guards you deem necessary on both doors. There is to be no access to General Eastbrook except to provide food and housekeeping by my personal servants until further notice."

"It will be done Your Majesty," Peters said stiffly still standing in the official army version of "at ease".

Perry smiled to himself. Both of them were playing their roles to near perfection. Peters was ready for the next level of command. He hoped whoever took over as General would recognize this and promote him.

The apartment at the top of the tower was opulent but a bit dusty. For a man who usually found comfort at night on a cot in a drafty tent it was a bit much. He did have a ranch which was very comfortable. But those were the practical comforts of a well to do farmer not an aristocrat. Perry was a frugal practical man.

The apartment had a definite feminine quality to it. Perry had heard rumors of Olivia's grandfather keeping a mistress close by. He decided this is what the apartment had been last used for. It was a short walk down the hallway from the king's chambers.

Perry had settled in for the night when a bookcase in the bedroom suddenly clicked, swung out, and then off to one side. To his surprise he locked eyes with Bria who hesitated then ran over and jumped up into his arms hugging him fiercely. Olivia followed with a troubled smile on her face and hugged him just as fiercely when Bria was done.

Tearfully Olivia said, "I will pardon you as soon as I can."

"You have more important things to do my queen," Perry said with affection clearly evident. "I am deeply sorry to have put you in this situation. I am even sorrier that I felt compelled to violate my oaths and murder your father."

"I'm not going to tolerate apologies or regrets on your behalf," Olivia said in her queenly voice. "You have done the people of this kingdom a great service. Your oath was to the realm, not to a man who was violating his oath to protect its people. The realm owes you more than it could ever repay."

Olivia hesitated to gather her thoughts and then said softly, "I am sorry my father is dead; he was my father. My mother was a saint, but my father was thoroughly evil. Opening up his 'hobby room' ended any doubts I might have had about that. My parents' arranged marriage was a terrible match. I believe he killed my mother for daring to oppose him. Justice has been delivered." At that point Olivia lost her composure and burst into tears. Bria wrapped her in a hug until the tears subsided.

They walked out into the richly appointed parlor with both Olivia and Bria wiping away tears and sat down. Perry waited until Olivia had composed herself and then said, "you need to get Prince Justin here as soon as possible. He's an expert in political intrigue and you're going to need his advice. I know you don't know him well. Your father was always worried the two of you would conspire against him. He forced the separation which is why you don't have a close relationship with him. I know him well; he's a good man. You can trust him."

"I'll pardon you both and then we can figure out what to do together," Olivia said.

"You should not give out any pardons until you fully understand the political situation. In fact, you're likely going to have to sacrifice one of us. Prince Justin is worth far more than I am. You own the most powerful army on the planet and there are several officers who can keep the peace on Liberty. Colonel Fedral would be an excellent choice. Politics are another matter. Things could spin completely out of control if the Commonwealth is involved. And I think they are. The first threat is civil war breaking out. The bigger threat is invasion by Arista. The best defense against that is a political solution with the Commonwealth," Perry said. He stopped for a moment and then asked, "I assume the hidden stairway comes up from the king's quarters, correct?"

"Yes, mom showed it to me when I was eight. She wanted me to know about all the hidden passageways in the castle so I could hide or escape if needed. She even showed me the hidden door to the 'hobby room' but told me to never go in there. It connects to a tunnel that leads outside the castle. I showed Bria and thought you ought to know of its existence," Olivia said. "We can use it to escape if necessary."

Perry nodded his head and said, "my advice is to limit your trips here. Reserve them for emergencies. I know it sounds paranoid, but you don't want any evidence supporting an accusation that you were involved in a conspiracy to kill the king. This is a deadly game Olivia. You should also have Justice Reynolds officially question Bria. Once he declares her innocent of knowledge or involvement you can resume spending time with her. Until then keep her confined to her rooms under guard."

"Dad no!" Bria said. "Olivia needs my support."

"It's only for a day or two and it's necessary to protect you both," Perry said.

Olivia had lots of questions which Perry did his best to answer. When the question-and-answer session fizzled away she said, "I'll have your military library brought up here. Can't imagine how you find that stuff interesting but it's probably better than sending up my romance novels," she said smiling. Then she handed him a dagger and said, "I don't want you weaponless Uncle Perry." It was the same dagger he had used to kill the king.

Perry was struck once again with Olivia's intelligence and empathy. Giving him that dagger was a clear signal that she fully supported him and what he had done. She knew he would be second guessing his actions. Perry replied, "probably not necessary, but thanks."

Olivia and Bria said their goodbyes and then shedding a few tears left the same way they came. Perry found the cleverly hidden bookcase door lock and engaged it. They would have to knock next time.

Two weeks went by with no news. Servants had

been instructed not to talk to him so he couldn't even question them on the common news of the day. He knew this was for their protection as well as the queens. For a man of action this was a hellish life.

Deep into an ancient text describing the care and maintenance of catapults there was a loud knock on the door. One of the guards called out, "you have visitors General Eastbrook."

"Enter," Perry said. He put his book down wondering what this was all about.

The queen, Justice Reynolds, Colonel Fedral, and Captain Peters walked in. The queen had an amused look on her face and said, "General Eastbrook. Will you please instruct Colonel Fedral to relinquish Prince Justin and his castle to my control?"

Perry was flabbergasted. He had assumed Fedral would recognize the situation and open the gates to the queen's authority. He should have known better. Colonel Fedral was an excellent administrator. He was an inspired battlefield commander matched only by Perry himself. He was also uncompromisingly loyal and incredibly stubborn. His orders had been to control the castle and protect Prince Justin until Perry ordered him otherwise.

"If I ever had any small doubts about you following orders they have been eliminated." Perry said to Fedral with a slow shake of his head and amusement in his eyes.

Colonel Fedral looked a little hurt and said, "yes sir."

"You are to follow all commands and orders given to you by Queen Olivia. Even if they countermand orders I have given you in the past."

"I understand sir," Colonel Fedral said simply. Then he turned to the queen and said, "I'm ready for your instructions Your Majesty. My deepest apologies for not following your earlier commands."

Queen Olivia looked him in the eyes and with a sincere voice said, "I value loyalty Colonel. Those who follow orders regardless of their difficulty are highly valued. It's a rare man who would stand firm given the situation you were put in. You handled it admirably. Thank you for all your contributions to the realm."

Fedral visibly relaxed and with pink cheeks said, "thank you Ma'am."

Olivia is going to be a wonderful leader thought Perry smiling inside.

"Colonel Fedral, you are promoted to General and are in charge of the Royal Armed Forces as of this moment onward. I would like Prince Justin to be brought under heavy guard to the royal castle as soon as practical. You should delegate that task as I have immediate need of your advice. We have quite a bit of planning to do."

General Fedral nodding his head turned to Peters and said "Captain, please use your Rangers for the prisoner transfer. Prince Justin is to be treated with all the respect and honors due a member of the royal family. Name a temporary replacement for yourself to head up castle security. I would also like you to carry orders for Coronel Pike and the army currently occupying the prince's castle. We'll bring the siege team back and have them take up a defensive position near the mountain pass north of the Royal Castle. I will have orders ready for you within the hour. When you return we'll discuss next steps."

"Yes sir," said Captain Peters

Turning back to the queen General Fedral said, "might I request regular access to General Eastbrook for advice on next steps for the Royal Armed Forces?"

"That is granted with the provision that Justice Reynolds is present at these meetings. No discussion of events associated with the rebel surrender or murder of the king are allowed," the queen said calmly. She then turned to Perry and said, "we'll leave you to your contemplations General Eastbrook." She hesitated a mere moment and let some warmth in her eyes show. She then exited confidently through the doorway radiating royalty.

After the door closed Perry allowed himself a smile of pride. She was already better at schooling her features. Even that last glance was done in a way that only he could see. Perry gave a deep sigh and was once again left to his books and his thoughts.

CHAPTER 9

# GOVERNOR'S UPDATE

Jack walked into the Governor's office wondering if this was his last hour of life. It had been a mistake to apply for First Minister in this sector. His career had been on a steep upward trajectory. His father had certainly played a role in his decision. "Jack, you don't reach the heights of Commonwealth administration by playing it safe," his father counseled.

"I've heard she's brutal and unforgiving. The last First Minister simply disappeared," Jack had said.

"Her next assignment is likely going to be on the High Council Jack. She's ticked all the boxes and been incredibly effective while doing so. Revenues from that sector have doubled, and they will double again before she is done. You might not like her, but it's a chance to gain a mentor destined to go far," his father had concluded.

And so, Jack had taken the risk. It had been a poor choice. As he was called into the Governor's office he decided he would face this with courage. He might as well go out in style. So, in keeping with that theme, he would stay calm, state the facts, and hope he survived.

"Good morning Jack, I hope you have good news," the governor said in greeting. It was maddening that she always greeted him with that statement. It made giving her bad news even worse. He suspected that was her intent.

"King Kenneth is dead, and his daughter is now queen. He was murdered by General Eastbrook. The mercenary army has been eliminated. My plan is in complete ruin," Jack said simply.

The Governor face showed a cold smile. Jack decided she wasn't going to swish her tail and walk away this time. Then she said, "what did you learn Jack?"

Jack hesitated, opened his mouth to speak, and then decided to think this through before answering. Turning this into a mentoring session was not what he expected. A small hope blossomed. Then he took a deep breath and said, "there were too many unpredictable players involved. I should have reduced the plan's reliance down to fewer people and ensured they had no option but to follow the plan exactly as laid out. King Kenneth deviated from the plan by ordering one of his Lords to take over the surrender from General Eastbrook. My guess is that he wanted to accelerate the plan by eliminating Prince Justin and General Eastbrook in one stroke. General Eastbrook obviously figured this out. I should have remained in Liberty and ensured the king stayed on plan. I underestimated the General and this is unforgiveable. He is known to have wide-ranging surveillance capability. He is also known to have exceptional judgement on military strategy and implementation," Jack said. Then he stopped and waited for judgement.

He felt good about his delivery. The Governor liked her summaries simple and to the point. No excuses and clear accountability. King Kenneth had actually changed the plan twice. First he agreed to a surrender negotiation, which in Jacks mind was an improvement. One of Jacks hidden flaws was that he did not approve of killing women and children. Sometimes it was necessary, but something he would avoid if possible. Then, unforgivably, the king actually tried to ambush General Eastbrook while he was with his army. This is a man who had successfully countered those types of attempts innumerable times. Sheer stupidity.

The Governors icy voice brought him back to the present. "What about Lord Druango?"

"While he has the right motivations for us to work with, he failed completely in carrying out the king's altered plan.

He should have either ensured success or refused to do it. I would not advise having him in a role where we're relying on his judgement," Jack said.

"So, he's one of the plans dependances that should have been worked around?" She asked.

"Yes Governor," Jack said simply.

"Who's fault is this disaster?" She asked.

"Mine entirely Governor," Jack responded.

Then she just stared at him with those mismatched cat eyes. Were the claws coming out he wondered. Maintaining eye contact was difficult but he knew that showing weakness was deadly. So, he looked back respectfully and waited for her to speak.

After what seemed like a lifetime she said, "you're right about the unforgiveable nature of underestimating Eastbrook."

"Yes ma'am," was all Jack said, stomach roiling.

Then she stared some more and finally said, "you know I'm not a forgiving person Jack."

"No ma'am," Jack said staying expressionless. She likes playing with her food he thought grimly.

After another long and uncomfortable silence, she asked, "so how do you propose to fix this situation?"

A thin ray of hope emerged once more with that question. But Jack knew he was still in a very dangerous position. "I do have a suggestion. It pushes Lord Druango into a support role and reduces the number of people we rely on," Jack said.

"What about timing?" She said. "You know my patience is wearing thin."

This was dangerous. His plan would take time to properly coordinate all the pieces. If he promised results on too aggressive of a schedule it might be his final act. Taking a deep breath, he said, "It adds 9 to 12 months to the timeline.

The risk of failure is lower and will be easier to administer in the long run."

She hesitated, smiled in all her cat glory, and purred, "come to my apartment tonight for dinner Jack. We'll discuss your new plan. We can also talk about how you are going to persuade me to allow your unforgiveable mistake." She then looked at him up and down openly and provocatively.

Jack's insides melted. He almost lost his composure and had to quickly lock down his facial expressions and body language. There were rumors about the Governor taking liberties with her staff. While she was commonly known as 'The Cat', she was also known in whispers as 'The Black Widow'. She was almost twice his age, although she didn't look it. Life extension therapies were readily available to the upper crust of Commonwealth citizens. Visibly a very attractive woman, her other attributes gave him the shivers. Her mismatched eyes would have been easy to fix with contacts or cosmetic surgery. Jack had come to believe she liked unsettling people. He wasn't sure he could do this, but he knew he didn't have a choice.

"What time should I arrive Governor?" he asked.

"Seven o'clock," she said with a sly smile. Then she slowly looked him up and down provocatively once more. "You can call me Julie in private Jack."

"I'll see you at seven Julie," Jack said as he forced what he hoped looked like an authentic smile and returned her provocative look.

As he walked out of her office Jack was torn on whether this was a good outcome or not. His best-case scenario going in was leaving with his life. A life whose career was destroyed, destined to die of boredom in a low-level job. But alive. Of the three options that might have been the best result. Leaving with his life was a pleasant surprise, but becoming the Governors latest toy was at best highly perilous.

# CHAPTER 10

# WEDDING NEGOTIATIONS

Olivia wished she could work closely with Perry and her uncle on the negotiations. Lord Durango had the backing of a minority group of Earls, Barons, and other wealthy landowners who mostly represented the two kingdoms recently subjugated in the Unification Wars. While she had the loyalty of the largest army on the planet, another civil war could weaken Liberty to the point of being an attractive target for Arista.

Lord Druango stood as Olivia entered the dreary meeting room set aside for her negotiations with him. "Good morning Your Majesty, you look very pretty today," the old, fat, and indolent man said as he looked her up and down provocatively.

It made her skin crawl. How was she going to be strong enough to do this? She decided leering at her was all part of an attempt to intimidate her. "Good morning Lord Druango," she said crisply.

He waited for her to sit and then sat himself and said with a sly smile, "your father made a wise decision arranging our betrothal. It is the best move to solidify unification of the realm and provide long-term stability for the royal family. Everyone needs to put down their swords and forget the divisions of the past."

Olivia smiled grimly back letting him know she wasn't intimidated and said, "now that I am queen I have no obligation to continue with this betrothal. If you really believe in unification then you will support pardons for Prince Justin and General Eastbrook. The evidence of the king's betrayal of the people of Liberty is compelling. People would rise up if either of them were punished," Olivia said forcefully.

"Opening the king's hobby room left little doubt as to his horrendous crimes. But, as you know there is still division within the kingdom. While I believe both of them would support the royal family without question, I'm not convinced safety for the people of my province would be protected. There are rumors that Arista is contacting influential people in an attempt to convince them life under their rule would be better. As Queens Consort I could be persuaded those fears are misplaced. If I am persuaded, I can persuade others who hold doubts. It's to everyone's benefit if we keep Arista out of Liberty," he said with a triumphant smile.

She did not believe his arguments had anything to do with a concern for people in his province. The tone of Druango's voice made it clear that being Lord of Druango worked equally well under Arista as under her as queen. This Lord was very good at making threats without saying anything that could be called treasonous. It was purely a power play. Unfortunately, House of Lords support for the pardons was a trump card. Without their support, civil war was highly likely. It was an excruciating decision. It meant sacrificing any hope of personal happiness for the good of the kingdom. She was confident the combination of Perry and her uncle would protect her from Durango's control. But Druango would have to be watched very closely. It wouldn't be a happy life. Having grown up knowing she would marry for the good of the kingdom, she had already accepted sacrifice as her fate. "I am willing to continue our betrothal once both Prince Justin and General Eastbrook's pardons are publicly supported by the entire House of Lords." Olivia had

Lord Druango locked eyes with her in a flinty glare and said, "I have no problem with pardoning both given we consummate a marriage as previously arranged. However General Eastbrook has been quite vocal in stating he wants to retire from the Army to go live on his ranch. I would expect you to ensure he does exactly that and doesn't interfere politically."

His suggestive emphasis on the word consummate made her skin crawl once more. Regardless, she couldn't let it affect her decision. The demand to exile Perry to his ranch had Olivia in turmoil. The one person of power she knew and trusted was Perry. Her experiences with General Fedral were good, but she didn't have a high level of trust built up yet. Perry had been vocal and public with his declarations of retiring to his ranch once the wars were over. He cast himself as a modern-day Cincinnatus who simply wanted to return to being a farmer. She knew the real reason for these declarations was to shore up the succession. General Eastbrook was wildly popular broadly across the realm. If he even breathed a desire to rule, the kingdom would be his. She knew Durango was trying to divide and conquer but she could always rescind Perry's exile if needed. Steeling herself to her fate she said, "I accept your conditions. I will pardon both and expect you to provide public support from the House of Lords before we are married."

"Done. I look forward to an expeditious wedding," he said smiling.

She nodded her head, got up and walked towards the door. As she did so she was very conscious of him staring at her body once more. God give me the strength to actually do this, she thought as she left the room.

On her walk down the hall to her uncle's accommodations she steeled herself for the anger Prince Justin would have for her decisions. She walked into Prince Justin's suite and said, "It's good to see you out of the dungeon uncle."

Prince Justin was clearly anxious when she walked in. His look was clearly asking for her to explain how her negotiations had gone. Exhaling some of the stress away she said, "It's done. I agreed to all of the concessions we discussed."

Prince Justin was visibly angry as predicted. He looked at her and shouted, "are you out of your mind Olivia! Lord Druango is evil and dangerous as a snake. He was going to murder me, Perry, and the families of everyone who opposed his plan with the king. He directed those mercenaries to kill children, CHILDREN!" Justin paused to control his anger then continued, "Lord Barlow's confession was coerced so not admissible in a trial. But that doesn't matter since he conveniently died in an accident."

"Well, I didn't say I expected him to be a good husband," she said sarcastically as she smiled back.

"This is not a time for jokes Olivia. Both Perry and I would be honored to be sacrificed for the good of the realm. I am not necessary, but Perry can ensure the regions stay loyal. The common people love him. The rest won't dare defy his army." He stopped a moment to collect himself and then said in a pleading voice, "I understand you need to marry for the good of the realm, but not that man!"

Olivia expression changed from amused to warmly stern and said, "you are my only insurance. Lord Durango won't kill me before I produce an heir. He won't do this because he knows you are next in line to assume the throne if I die childless. He also knows you will be Regent if he kills me after I have produced an heir. With you out of the picture he has an easy pathway to the throne. Fedral is an excellent General, but he can't insure loyalty like Perry can."

"I hate this decision," Prince Justin said. Then he sat down and moved his glance from her to the floor pouting like a child.

Olivia smiled, patted him arm and said, "you are the Queens Advisor. I expect you to tell me when you think I'm making poor decisions. I will always listen and consider what you say. But, when I decide I expect you to honor my decisions and do your best to implement them. I have made this decision."

"Don't worry about my loyalty, never worry about that. I will support your decisions." Justine took a deep breath and said, "on another topic, I am also not happy with the plan to exile Perry. Fedral does not have the same level of respect and loyalty from the common soldiers that Perry does. Everyone knew your father was a horrible king but once Perry declared his intent to honor his oath most unquestioningly backed him. They think of him as one of their own. We need his leadership," Prince Justin pleaded.

"That was a very difficult decision. I agree we need his council and leadership. But having him in the castle is detrimental in the short term. The minority in the House of Lords will be more defiant with him around. He defeated most of them in battle. They remember being his prisoner. If a crisis breaks out I can rescind the exile order and bring him back," Olivia said.

"His ranch is remote. We need to make sure he has a lot of security around him," Prince Justin counseled.

"I agree about the need for security. Durango and his minions would love nothing more than an accident at the ranch. I was thinking of asking him to step down and become commander of the Rangers instead of retirement. He came up through those ranks and there isn't anyone better to train and organize them. His ranch is conveniently located near strategic roads connecting the three regions. Easy to argue it's a good place for an army camp. He will be living on his ranch as agreed, but this would essentially give him a good-sized elite army at his disposal. I discussed it with General Fedral, and he agrees. To be honest, Fedral believes all of this is subterfuge. In his opinion he's still Perry's second in command. We've discussed promoting Captain Peters by jumping Major directly to Lt Colonel and making him Perry's second in command," Olivia explained.

"He seems awfully young," Prince Justin said.

"Believe it or not he has 15 years' experience in the Royal

Army. Peters was an orphan and lied about his age at 13 to join the army. His motivation was literally to avoid starvation. He rose up the non-commissioned ranks quickly because of his fighting skills, judgement, and intelligence. Perry saw something special in him and eventually gave him a battlefield promotion to commissioned officer. Fedral told me this is extremely rare. I think Perry identifies with him. They both came from poverty and they both came up through the ranks. Peters certainly worships the ground Perry walks on. They have a high level of personal trust. I can't think of a better bodyguard. Especially since Perry won't accept a bodyguard," Olivia said smiling.

"You are definitely sneaky enough to be queen, Your Majesty," Prince Justin said with a touch of light sarcasm and the first smile of the day.

"I wish sneaky wasn't something I needed to be good at. Would prefer to just be honest with everyone. The days of simplicity are unfortunately gone forever," she said with a sad expression on her face.

Next stop was Bria. She kept very few secrets from her best friend. Bria had encouraged her to keep her father's fate a secret until it was decided. It wasn't a selfish request; her motivation was a belief that it would make it easier on Olivia. Bria was truly a gift from heaven, Olivia thought. In her world of royal politics Bria was the one person her age who loved her. Bria only desired love and friendship in return. They had solemnly sworn as small girls to always stay close.

She walked into Bria's quarters and said smiling, "I have good news, your father has been pardoned."

Bria hesitated in answering studying her closely. "And?" Bria asked locking eyes with her.

"You know me too well," Olivia said with a touch of sadness in her voice. "The 'and' is that I have to exile him to the ranch for now. You can go live with your father on the ranch just like you always wanted."

Surprisingly, Bria smiled and said, "unless you exile me

too I'm staying here."

"But you've always said you want to live near your father. That the wars have robbed you both of time together," Olivia argued with a furrowed brow.

"Dad and I already discussed it. You are going to need someone to talk to who cares about you. That would be me," Bria said with a smirk.

Olivia couldn't help but smile, then she said in surprise, "how did he find out he was going to be exiled."

"He told me when he first got here that you would negotiate pardons with Lord Druango. He told me the right move would be to sacrifice him and break your engagement with Lord Druango. In his opinion you are predictably guilty of letting your heart win out over your head," Bria said with a knowing smile. "We agreed if his prediction came true I would stay close to help you. Dad is really worried about you Olivia. We both are," Bria said.

"I'm glad your dad is a friend and not an enemy Bria. He's endearing but it's scary how well he predicts what people are going to do," Olivia said as she started to relax. One of her big fears was that Bria would be offended by Olivia's treatment of her father. That she would move to the ranch with Uncle Perry and cut off communication.

"Dad told me to give you a suggestion in case 'you insist on making bad decisions'. He suggests you build a summer house on the ranch. He said you could visit your Uncle Perry during the hot muggy season when the House of Lords is not in session," Bria said with a hopeful expression.

"God, that's a wonderful idea! I loved the ranch when we were girls," Olivia said with brightness glowing in her eyes.

"It's a bit rough Olivia. I'm not sure you're remembering it accurately," Bria said smiling.

"Those were the happiest days of my life Bria. After my mother died the castle was gloomy and filled with people who either saw me as an opportunity or an annoyance. The ranch was beautiful. My best friend was there. No courtiers.

Just real people who cared about me. Aunt Beatrice was fussing over me and making me laugh instead of being surrounded by servants with cold smiles. I had work to do. Taking care of the animals and working in the fields was very satisfying. A home on the ranch where I can stay part of the year sounds like heaven," Olivia said wistfully. Then with her face transforming into a grin she said, "Where else can I practice my knife throwing."

They both laughed, stood up, and hugged each other fiercely. Like Olivia, Bria was an only child whose mother had died when she was young. While growing up she was either on the ranch, at the castle, or on a campaign. When he had a choice, arguments to leave Bria behind simply didn't work with her father. Wherever he went, she went. Exposed to the dangers of war, and the castle, Perry decided she needed to be able to protect herself. The problem was that Bria was incredibly soft hearted. She refused to hit anyone or spar with weapons. "What if I hurt someone," she had exclaimed in horror to her father.

"That's the whole point Bria," he responded with obvious exasperation.

"Well then I won't do it," she declared and then locked her face into her well-known look of absolute determination. In addition to being soft hearted, Bria was the most stubborn person on the planet according to her father. Frustrated, Perry finally got her to throw knives by turning it into a friendly game. They would compete with a set of throwing knives and a wooden target they took everywhere. Olivia had gotten into the act on an early visit to the ranch and turned out to have natural skill. She always beat Bria, which wasn't hard because Bria didn't care. But she also won regularly against Uncle Perry. This delighted both girls. Mostly because it frustrated the extremely competitive Uncle Perry. Making it even better, Perry's staff had gotten into the act by ribbing him about it when the girls were around.

Olivia took a deep breath, let it out, and then said, "Would you have an early breakfast with me tomorrow? The wedding is at noon, and I would love to have lots of time to get ready together."

"Of course. How about we both wear our special hair pins," Bria proposed with a grin "Only father will know what they are, and he'll smile when he sees them."

Their hair pins were cleverly disguised throwing knives. They were small but made of an extremely dense wood that maintained an edge. They were also heavy enough to penetrate deeply when thrown. Their decorative carved and painted sheaths successfully hid their purpose. Perry had gifted them both with the matching hair pin knives years ago. They had worn them to many royal events in the past. Given their close friendship it wouldn't look inappropriate at the wedding.

"I love that idea. Gloria will hate it, but she'll go along if I insist," Olivia said smiling. Gloria was the royal interior designer and dresser for Olivia. Arguably the most beautiful woman in the realm. She had a warm personality and was blessed with an eye for color and excellent taste. "I wish your dad could give me away," Olivia continued. "But politically it has to be Prince Justin. Nothing against him, but I really don't know him all that well."

"If there was ever someone who deserves a fairy tale ending it's you. Unfortunately, it looks like you're only going to get the best friend and her father part of the story," Bria said with a sad smile which Olivia returned. The two best friends spent the evening sipping wine and reminiscing about their lives knowing it was all about to change forever. As Olivia left Bria's apartment she thought once again that she would gladly walk away from wealth and luxury for freedom. Freedom to live her life the way she chose. For her, there was little liberty on Liberty. She had pardoned her uncle that morning and would pardon Perry this evening.

The morning of the wedding Bria was modeling Olivia's wedding dress when a loud commotion broke out in the hallway. The door burst open, and a rough looking man ran in with blood dripping off the sharp edges of his sword. He smiled cruelly when he saw Bria and as he hurried towards her he said, "you're coming with me queeny."

Bria froze not knowing what to do. There was a loud clash of swords in the hallway. It sounded like the fight was getting closer. She feared that meant the queen's guards were being overwhelmed. "I said you're coming with me," he said in an angry voice as he advanced towards Bria.

As he got close a knife suddenly appeared in his neck. He fell and was spilling his life out on the marble floor when Bria turned and saw Olivia standing angry and defiant with her hair now loose and flowing over her shoulders.

Pushing down the bile in her throat she forced herself into action. Bria found her voice and said firmly, "Olivia, the apartment!"

Olivia hesitated, then nodding her head ran over to a bookcase. She released a hidden catch and swung the hidden door open. She motioned Bria over and when Bria didn't move she refused to enter alone. Bria ran quickly over and surprised Olivia by pushing her hard into the stairway landing beyond. Bria pushed the hidden door closed. She quickly found the lock and heard it click just before more of the invaders entered the queen's dressing room.

"Grab her and let's get out of here before we have to fight off the entire Royal Army." The oldest of the men said. One of the larger men jogged over, grabbed her roughly, and threw a hood over her head. He picked her up and slung her over his shoulder. For the second time she fought down the urge to throw up. The vision of blood pulsing out of the first man's neck kept running through her mind.

"Hey, grab the pretty one too. She'll be worth something," the one in charge ordered.

Bria heard Gloria wail out an agonized protest about her children. Her heart sank even further thinking about the two beautiful little twin girls who visited sometimes. It was horrific to contemplate their grief. These men were slavers. They hadn't been active in Liberty for decades given the planet's large army and rich kingdoms. The retribution Liberty could extract wasn't worth it. Bria was terrified but proud she had saved Olivia from this fate. They had obviously targeted the queen as part of a plan likely cooked up by Lord Durango. If they didn't find a queen then they would keep looking, and Bria couldn't risk that. Why now and not later? Bria couldn't figure out the logic. The castle was overflowing with armed men given the number of Lords and Ladies attending the wedding. She composed herself wondering what she should do. Then she remembered her father's voice repeating one of his oft quoted axioms 'never correct your enemy's mistakes'. They thought they had captured Queen Olivia. She would not correct their mistake.

CHAPTER 11

# VOYAGE

Tee was in the middle of his twice a day exercise routine. You would have to look very closely to notice muscles flexing and relaxing. He was careful to do it when the guards weren't present, and Theo was either sleeping or not paying attention to him. It was a lengthy and elaborate routine intended for use when Guard members were confined for multiple days in a small space. It was part of their scout training. The Guard wanted everyone to be prepared for just about anything. While it did not take the place of real exercise at least it raised the heart level a little and slowed down muscle atrophy.

Suddenly the door unlocked, opened, and two women were escorted in. They were each given orders to go into one of the two empty cells. When they didn't move quickly enough they were roughly shoved in. The one directly across from him was stunningly beautiful. She was terrified and Tee's heart went out to her. Fortunately, Theo was asleep, or she would already be suffering his verbal abuse. The second woman cross corner from Tee was also pretty but more athletic looking which appealed to Tee. She also exhibited a stoic nature against the rough treatment that radiated confidence. Another attractive quality. She examined both him and Theo carefully but without being obvious about it.

The woman across from him said, "hi, my name's Gloria. Do you know where we are?"

"Theron doesn't know. Theron wants to go home," Tee said staying in character.

"Oh dear," Gloria said with compassion in her voice. "Are you scared Theron?"

"Yes," Tee whispered. "Theron scared of Theo," Tee said pointing towards the other prisoner and cringing away from him at the same time.

"He's simple Gloria. I can't believe they would put someone like him in a cage," Bria said softly but with a clear tinge of anger in her voice.

The tone in Bria's voice woke up Theo. He rubbed his eyes, looked around, and smiled widely. "Well look at what we have here Theron, women for Theo." He stood up and moved to the bars to get as close a look as possible. Then he pointedly looked both over carefully. He turned toward Gloria and said "You know the guards owe me a favor. I'll get them to let us spend some time together in my cell. You know there is only one thing women are good for. Can you guess?" When she turned bright red he laughed harshly, started fondling himself. Then he proceeded to describe in disgusting detail what he thought women were good for.

"Leave her alone," Bria demanded.

Theo turned to her and smiled his evil smile and said, "you must be jealous of the attention I'm giving the pretty one. You're not bad yourself. You know the guards owe me more than one favor. After I'm done with her we can spend a little time together too."

"You touch either one of us and I'll kill you," Bria said coldly. She knew it was an empty promise. Hurting people was not something she could bring herself to do. Silly to threaten anyway.

"I'm not someone you want to threaten. After I'm done with you, you'll plead for death. That's a promise," Theo said coldly with his smile still in place.

Bria turned towards Gloria. "Ignore him Gloria. He's locked up just like we are. You're safe from him," Bria said soothingly. Then she shot a quick cold smile at Theo and turned away. Gloria took her cue from Bria, turned away and seemingly ignored Theo's continued descriptions of their future activities together.

In the middle of what Tee had decided was night the door unlocked and then was slammed open. Three guards stumbled in. Tee could smell the alcohol. Staying in character he cringed on his narrow bed with his knees held in a fetal position.

"I told you they were beautiful," Smelly said slurring his words.

"Meant for some Senators entertainment no doubt. I like this one," the older of the two new guards said pointing at Bria.

"No! She's special. Queen of Liberty no less, and a certified virgin to boot," Smelly said firmly. We're worse than dead if we touch that one.

"Will we be in trouble with this one," the new guard with buck teeth said pointing at Gloria.

"We've been told to be careful with all of them." Smelly looked at Gloria lustfully and swaying a bit said, "she's had kids so nothing special other than being beautiful. She's only in here because they were worried the men in the holding cell would all want a go at her and damage the goods. As long as we're careful nobody will care."

"Don't touch her," Bria shouted at them.

"Shut up bitch. You're lucky you're special or I would give you to Theo for entertainment," Smelly said. Then he opened Glorias cell and as they entered Tee shut his eyes tightly. It was in character for him to turn away and shut his eyes. Tee simply could not watch what was obviously going to happen next.

The next hour was a nightmare. Gloria was crying and pleading for them to stop. Bria was shouting obscenities. And Theo was offering suggestions of what the guards should do next. Tee was sick to his stomach and enraged that anyone could abuse another human being like this. When Glorias crying weakened into whimpering Tee started to hope they were finally finished with her.

"Well, that was fun. Can we do this again," Buck Tooth said as the door to Gloria's cell clanked shut.

"It will take a couple of weeks to complete all the jumps to Arista," Smelly said chuckling. "We have to be careful not to get caught. But we'll have lots of time with her."

"Hey, how about you let me have some time with her. There are suggestions I was keeping to myself that you might enjoy watching," Theo said with hope in his voice.

"No. You're not leaving that cell until we get to Arista," Smelly said sounding like he was sobering up. He turned to the other two guards and said, "This disgusting excuse for a human being loves to torture and kill people. He likes to do it slowly. They are going to use his skills at the Arena. The emperor likes that sort of thing to start the games. He's only in here because he would damage the goods if he were in the holding cells."

"If you won't let me have a go at her, how about letting Theron provide a bit more entertainment," Theo said chuckling.

"That's not a bad idea." Buck Tooth said. "A video might make a little extra money on the black market. There are people into all kinds of weird shit."

"No way we let that monster out of his cell," Old Guy said.

"He's a moron you idiot. The extraction team fucked up big time and heads are going to roll. He's still in this section because he's from Pacifica and has value in the arena. I can only imagine what they will do to him. We might as well have a little fun while we have the chance. I think it could be worth a few credits," Smelly said smiling.

Bria started in with insults and obscenities again as Tee heard his cell door unlock. He opened his eyes and said, "Theron wants to stay here," in a pleading voice. He could see the guards visibly relax and then smile in anticipation.

"Help me get him into her cell," Smelly said, motioning to Buck Tooth, and then he said. "We're probably going to have to help him figure it out." They all chuckled.

Bria was more disgusted than she had ever been in her life. She had heard stories of rape. She had been warned to be aware of her surroundings from a young age. She even knew women it had been rumored to have happened to. But she never thought there were people so sick as to do the things she had just witnessed. And now this! She watched the guards guide the huge simpleton out of his cell. Smiling and cracking jokes they roughly pushed him along. Hunched over and whimpering, he timidly allowed them to guide him toward Glorias cell door.

When all three of the Guards were within arm's length the simpleton transformed. To her horror, in the blink of an eye, all three guards were on the floor and appeared to be dead. Blood was pooling beneath them. The simpleton had turned into a killing machine. It happened so quickly Bria couldn't quite understand what had just happened. Once she did, she vomited violently and quickly backed up away from her cell door terrified by what she had just witnessed.

"Don't be afraid. I'm not going to hurt you," Tee said to Gloria as she stood glued to the back wall of her cell. He stood erect, confident, and calm with a soothing voice. His eyes had transformed from vacant to warmly penetrating. He took one step towards Gloria then stopped when she squealed in terror cowering. Turning to Bria he said softly, "Why don't I unlock your cell, and you can help her."

"Don't come near me," Bria said firmly but in a quavering voice.

"Hey tough guy, how about letting me out to comfort her if Her Majesty doesn't want to," Theo said.

Tee bent down and relieved Smelly of his keys. Then he calmly walked over and unlocked Theo's cell door. As Tee entered Theo suddenly lost his macho attitude and feinted to one side then attacked. Just as blazingly fast as before Theo was dead on the floor after having his head bashed against the wall. Bria vomited again from the sight of Theo's brains stuck on the wall but starting to dribble down to collect on the floor. Tee then calmly dragged the three guards into Theo's cell and covered them with Theo's sheets. He locked Theo's cell door then turned to Bria. "Don't throw whatever it is in your hair at me." Hesitating, he locked eyes with her and said, "If I harm you or Gloria in any way you have my permission to kill me." Then he walked into his cell, locked the door, and threw all the keys to Bria. "There, I hope that helps you feel a little safer. You should get Gloria over to your cell. She is in shock and needs someone to help her." He stopped for a moment and then said with a grim smile. "I prefer to be called Tee by the way."

Bria was in shock, and it took a few moments to compose herself. She had to gather her courage before venturing over to guide Gloria back to her cell.

"Can we have a little privacy please," Bria said in a sharp tone.

"Anytime. All you have to do is ask but please let me know when you're done," Tee answered.

As far as Bria could tell, Gloria didn't have any permanent physical damage. Emotional damage was a whole other matter, especially given Gloria's history. She couldn't imagine Gloria escaping from what she had experienced in her life without permanent scars. Bria wasn't sure she herself would ever escape the horror of the last hour. As she gently cleaned up Gloria she stole glances at Tee. No longer bent over or cringing. He appeared to be honestly concerned for them. He was handsome and this new version of him had kind intelligent eyes. Seemingly blessed with an easy manner, Bria could imagine him being very attractive to most woman. However, Bria couldn't get past the Jekyll and Hyde transformation. The sudden change from a harmless simpleton to the deadliest thing she had ever seen terrified her to her core. She had been completely fooled by Theron the simpleton. Was this new version just another masterful acting performance? She decided to be wary of Tee. To watch him carefully. The fact he had known she had a weapon and was considering using it was almost magical. Yes, she would watch him carefully.

A few hours later another guard unlocked the door, walked in, and froze. Eyes wide he quickly turned and ran out locking the door behind him. Tee could hear yelling in the hallway beyond. Tee allowed a grin to surface as he imagined the discussions. He glanced back over at Bria again, worried he had gone too far. He had broken training. He wasn't sorry he'd done it. There was no way he was going to continue to play a role waiting for an opportunity to escape. He had been enraged and thoroughly disgusted by the three guards. But that wasn't why he killed them. The women needed protection. What he had done was the only way he knew to protect them against these particular guards and Theo. She surely understood justice had been served. Anyone that would do what was done to Gloria didn't deserve to live. She hadn't yet heard Theo's stories of what he had done to countless men, women, and yes children. Somehow he knew Theo's stories were true, Tee felt he had an obligation to end Theo's horrendous abuse. More importantly, he felt an obligation to protect the two women from this collection of monsters.

The security officer for the ship was terrified. Three guards and a slave with highly valuable skills were dead. Worse, that particular slave had been personally requested by the emperor. The guards were his men, his responsibility. He had locked up the acquisition team on the captains' orders when their Pacifica captive turned out to be a simpleton. Laughing at them, he had explained that the captain wanted to make sure they lived long enough for their benefactor to decide what to do. He was remembering their evil grins as he took their place. He wished at least one of those three idiots had lived. Someone would have to pay the price for the lost revenue and the emperor's ire. He was the only one left.

CHAPTER 12

# PLUTA

A polite and efficient butler dutifully took the First Minister's hat and coat then escorted him to an austere but spacious office. "Thank you for seeing me on such short notice Magistrate," Jack said in greeting.

"Always happy to serve the Commonwealth," replied Pluta smiling. Pluta was a vigorous man in his sixties who took pride in his appearance. He had steely colored hair covering an intimidating face highlighted by dark penetrating eyes. He made most people uncomfortable. This was intentional.

Pluta didn't like the First Minister. He thought there was something undefinably soft about him. Weakness was a good thing in enemies or junior partners. But not in the person controlling the Commonwealths involvement in a delicate and lucrative endeavor. He had only met the Governor once. That was someone you could rely on to do what was necessary. Someone after his own heart, or lack thereof, he thought smiling grimly to himself.

"The Governor's plan has changed. We would like you to take on a larger role," Jack said.

"I don't like it when plans change," Magistrate Pluta said forcefully while staring at Jack. His philosophy was to negotiate all changes to a plan. His pretended outrage at proposed changes was heightened if he thought the other sides negotiator was weak. And he thought Jack was weak.

Jack locked eyes with him and calmly said, "I misspoke. Your continued involvement in this venture requires you to take on a larger role."

Magistrate Pluta had to collect himself before he said something he would regret. The gall of this insolent puppy to threaten his involvement in a scheme that was his idea. The First Minister was crucial to his future and had to be appeased. A subservient approach, however detestable, was required here. "My apologies First Minister. I did not mean to indicate I was unwilling to do whatever the Commonwealth requires. I just get concerned when plans change midstream."

"Understandable. This change is to your advantage Magistrate. The Governor has authorized an increase in your share of the tax revenue from this venture to twenty percent," Jack said.

Pluta was sure the First Minister had seen his shock at that news. He had allowed greed to show on his face. Pluta's share had just doubled! His original forecast from this venture was already astronomical. The First Minister had been clever in delivering the news. He might sense weakness in the man, but he needed to make sure he didn't underestimate him.

Jack let a knowing smile cross his face communicating that he had indeed noticed the reaction. He hesitated a moment to let that sink in and then said, "the Governor is proposing raising the stakes. We would like you to continue owning the Arista side of this and take over Lord Druango's role."

Pluta was confused and he let it show on his face. He shook his head slightly side to side and said, "you want me to marry the queen of Liberty?"

Jack laughed and said, "we want you to control the queen. You don't have to marry her yourself."

"How do you expect me to control the queen of Liberty," Pluta asked, his confusion deepening.

"By contracting with the slave ship to pick her up on their way back from Pacifica," Jack said continuing to smile.

"That would be extremely expensive. The emperor would have to approve. That is an act of war," Pluta said.

"The slave ship is an independent contractor as far as the Justice Ministry is concerned. They are authorized to capture slaves from any planet. As long as they sell them at a Commonwealth authorized public auction it's perfectly legal," Jack explained. "Liberty might declare war, but they are hardly in a position to do so. The whole planet is reeling from decades of war followed by a coup. In addition, General Eastbrook and Prince Justin have recently been pardoned for their roles in the coup dividing the planet further."

"I'll have to think about this," Pluta said. The shock of this news overwhelmed him.

"Think about the best way to control the queen. The slavers have already picked up the queen on your behalf. The acquisition cost will be deducted from the sale price at auction," Jack said, obviously enjoying putting Pluta on his back foot.

Pluta looked away from Jack so he could concentrate. He had invested heavily in slave acquisition ventures to the minor planets in the sector. The Justice Ministry had been bribed from his own coffers to allow the Pacifica acquisition. An accusation that the bribe included a stop on Liberty would stick. He was trapped. He had paid the bribe for the Pacifica captive to impress the emperor. Pluta enjoyed the blood and gore of the games. But he didn't enjoy it as much as the emperor. He would have to explain this was a major contribution to the emperor's plan to conquer Liberty.

Something the emperor loved to talk about. Yes it could be made to work. If it didn't, he might end up as entertainment at the Arena.

"I will talk to the emperor and get him on board with the new plan. When does the slave ship dock?" Pluta asked.

"Next week. As we agreed, communications on the slave ship schedule are locked down. The public auction can be as private as you would like it to be," Jack said smiling.

Pluta took pride in not underestimating people. He had underestimated the First Minister. He could see now why the young man had risen so fast in the Commonwealth. He wouldn't make that mistake again.

It was insane to make enemies of any citizen of the Commonwealth. Much less one who had power. It would be difficult, but he resolved to put this child in his place at some point. That enjoyment would have to wait. There was a lot to do. He would instruct the auction house to open very early in the morning and reverse the order of bidding. High value slaves first and then wait until normal business hours to sell the more common ones. Most bidders at the slave auctions were a late-night bunch. If news of the auction didn't leak he should be able to secure both the Pacifica fighter and the queen. As in chess, the queen was the key piece. What he would do with his queen was a mystery. But it was an exciting mystery to work out.

CHAPTER 13

# THE AUCTION

Someone was going to pay, thought Pluta seething in anger. A few minutes before the slave auction was to start Senator Cereo walked in. As usual he was attended to by his valet and security team. Pluta was jealous of Cereo's security team. They were six ex-gladiators who had all gained their freedom by winning the required thirty bouts. Pluta had tried bribing several of them over the years to no avail. Obviously, his own personal servants weren't adverse to bribes. Either that or the emperor was pitting them against each other. Cereo's presence at the auction was proof of foul play.

"Good morning Magistrate," Caius Cereo had greeted Pluta with a smile that didn't quite reach his eyes. "Looks like we both stumbled on this auction. They usually advertise them in advance." Caius was extremely charismatic. It required work to dislike him. It was a mistake to think he was just an unusually good salesman. What set him apart was that he rarely, if ever, made a bad business decision. This good judgement had followed him into the political arena where he had slowly become a serious threat to Pluta and his cronies.

"It is odd, isn't it. Unusual to see you this early in the morning Senator," Pluta said suggesting his presence might not have been accidental.

"Was just on my way home when I noticed the auction house doors opened. I decided to peek in," Caius said. "Do you know what they are auctioning this morning?"

"It's about to start so I guess we'll find out together," he lied. "Hopefully, something interesting. We have a senate hearing tomorrow. I look forward to seeing you then," Pluta said as he turned and walked to his bidding station.

The first slave they brought out was stunningly beautiful. One of the most beautiful women Pluta had ever seen. Pleasure slaves were usually brought out nude. This one was dressed in a sheer chemise that was cut low barely covering her breasts and high enough to show most of her legs. It left little doubt about what was underneath without actually showing it. The woman was attempting to cover herself, the cold room accentuating two of her attributes. One of the handlers barked a stern command for her to put her arms down. She flinched, clearly terrified of him. Eyes cast towards the floor she had tears streaming down her face. She was distraught, humiliated, and completely submissive to the instructions from her handlers.

"You won't find a prettier or more willing pleasure slave than this one. Already broken in, she will do anything you ask. Previously she was the Dresser for the queen of Liberty. She is experienced in interacting with nobility and can provide entertainment for those of the highest station. Bidding starts at five thousand credits," the auctioneer said.

Bidding was enthusiastic until it got to 15,000 credits. To Pluta's surprise Caius raised his hand and bid 20,000 credits. That silenced the other bidders, and the gavel was struck. As the woman was taken away he caught Caius's eye and gave him a knowing smile and nod. Caius just nodded back with the corners of his mouth slightly upturned.

Pluta was surprised. Caius had lots of slaves. All those of high station did. He kept the bulk of them on his massive villa properties where he had located the bulk of his agricultural and manufacturing businesses. Caius had few house slaves in Roma and didn't offer any of them for entertainment. This was unusual for someone of his wealth and station. One rumor was that he was prudish. His wife was from a common farm family. She went everywhere with him so perhaps he was under her control. Another possibility was that he was extremely paranoid about his security. None of his slaves were in residence at his Roma Domus for long.

He rotated them between Roma and his villa. Pluta had been unable to bribe any of Caius's house slaves. Threats hadn't worked either. As soon as he had one of them threatened, they disappeared. Presumably back to Caius's villa. His purchase of this woman gave him an idea. Perhaps Caius did have a weakness. Maybe he enjoyed pliant submissive pleasure slaves. Could he use this weakness to sneak a spy or even another assassin into Caius's villa? Something to consider.

Next up was the Pacifica Guard captive. He was brought out in heavy chains surrounded by a large team of rough looking handlers. Although the handlers looked tough, they also looked a little frightened of their charge. The small crowd naturally shrunk back a little. The man was massive, although Pluta thought he was smaller than expected. There was no fear in this man. Just a quiet confidence that radiated danger. When he looked at you, your instinct was to back up and look away. The primal threat was palpable.

"Next up we have the ultimate killing machine. This man was born and bred on Pacifica and his capture was authorized by the Justice Ministry for indigenous peoples' research. As anyone who loves the Arena knows, members of the Pacifica Guard are unequaled in combat. On the voyage here guards made a minor mistake in handling him with four dead as the result. The most challenging task you will have managing the star of your stable is finding credible opponents. Bidding starts at 100,000 credits."

A gasp came up from the small crowd with that announcement. A top tier gladiator usually topped out at 50,000 credits. However, it had been years since the Commonwealth had authorized capturing one of the Pacifica Guards and they were unique. Pluta knew the acquisition cost from the slavers was partially responsible for this exorbitant starting bid. He had expected this. Pluta started the bidding out at 100,000 credits and gritted his teeth hoping Caius wasn't interested. He was. They went back and forth until Pluta bid 150,000 credits. At that point, the auctioneer stopped the bidding.

"Apologies from the Auction house, but we need to pause for a few minutes to discuss the latest bid. Magistrate Pluta would you meet with me and the Import Minister at the auctioneer's table?"

Pluta stormed over to the auctioneers table intending on tearing this low-level slave dealer a new orifice. "What is your problem?" he said making it personal with the malice in his voice.

"I apologize for stopping the bidding, but you are 500 credits short of that bid in your account," the auctioneer said respectfully.

Pluta was stunned. The Commonwealth required all import and export transactions to be in cash. This was done so tax revenues could be immediately credited to the Commonwealth. His bidding account was tied to his main cash account at his bank. There were millions of credits in that account. He turned to the Import Minister and said, "can we delay bidding until I can get this straightened out with my bank?"

The Import Minister was unaffected by Pluta's demeanor. A representative of the Commonwealth had nothing to fear from a colonist no matter how rich and powerful. He calmly said, "no Magistrate. You know the Commonwealths rules. I've already allowed a minor violation by stopping the process to discuss this with you. It was a courtesy, nothing more. All planned sales have to be executed in a timely fashion once the bidding starts."

Pluta just nodded his head, turned, and rushed away to the communication portal supplied by the Commonwealth. He called his bank president's private line. "Why are automatic account transfers down this morning?" Pluta asked angrily without any attempt at a greeting.

The bank president had obviously been asleep when the call came in. He was clearly frightened as evidenced by the sweat starting to form on his brow. Pluta was his largest customer. "I'm sorry but the Commonwealths communications services company told us late yesterday they needed to shut down transfers for a few hours this morning. They said it was standard maintenance. We were told we'd be back online well in advance of normal business hours. I had no idea you would need a large transfer of cash so early in the morning."

"We'll discuss this later," Pluta said curtly and broke the Commonwealth provided connection. He was beside himself with frustration and anger. As he walked back into the auction room he remembered that Caius had an interest in a company that provided local communications support services for the Commonwealth. Few Commonwealth citizens wanted to suffer the inconvenience of living in the colonies. So, a limited number of carefully scrutinized locals were trained and contracted for services. Communications were completely controlled by the Commonwealth and could only be used for financial transactions and communications regarding them. This was allowed because it sped tax revenues to the Commonwealth. The bank had no control over the movement of money or the choice of when maintenance would be performed. The stranglehold the Commonwealth had on its colonists was oppressive.

Word had gotten out once bidding had started and the auction room was now starting to fill. As he got to his bidding station Queen Olivia was brought out. She was young, beautiful, and radiated health. The auction house had her decked out like the queen she was. Instead of provocative clothing, she had on a formal dress that would have been appropriate for a state function. They presented her with liveried handlers adding to her regal posture and attitude. She looked every bit the queen of a substantial kingdom as she looked disdainfully down onto the crowd. The auctioneer announced the start of bidding.

"In front of you is the queen of Liberty. As is well known, that kingdom is in disarray and a claim to the kingdom could be made by anyone who legally marries the queen. Of course, you have to do more than conquer her to do it." The sexual inuendo brought out a round of chuckles. It also pinked the queens' cheeks slightly, adding to her allure. "If you can legally marry and conquer the planet, Commonwealth recognition of legal ownership is assured. Bidding starts at 125,000 credits.

Caius raised his hand and called out in a clear voice "150,000." There was stunned silence as the other bidders considered his bid. On the one hand, ownership of the queen could be extremely lucrative. At the very least you could sell her back to Liberty for a fortune. On the other hand, it was extremely dangerous to play planetary politics. Anyone who had any sense at all was terrified of the Commonwealth. Driving up the price on something Senator Cereo clearly wanted was also a risk. If the emperor was somehow orchestrating this it was suicide. The other bidders considered their futures and decided to stay quiet.

"No other bids?" asked the auctioneer. "Sold to Senator Cereo for 150,000 credits."

Pluta left the auction house at once. It was a short walk to his office, and he set a fast pace. Surrounded by his security team he noticed they were keeping their gazes off of him. They were close enough to hear his conversations with both the auctioneer and the bank president. While his face and demeaner were controlled they understood what had happened. Anyone who worked for Pluta was terrified of getting on the wrong side of him.

When he reached his office he looked at his security team and said, "you are not to talk to anyone about this morning. Understood?" He looked at each of them in turn as they nodded their understanding.

There in his office he let his emotions run free. "Humiliating!" he yelled to himself. "I should have crushed him when I had the chance!" When upset he tended to talk to himself. Part of the reason his office was soundproof. Pluta wasn't one to obsess over the mistakes of the past. However, there was one mistake he regularly whipped himself over. Once more he punished himself by reviewing that horrible decision of thirty years ago.

He remembered being tired from long hours of work. His eyes had burned. He had been going over the accounts in his various businesses. As he completed that task he was re-energized knowing the next order of business was the final phase of a project he delighted in. Nothing was more satisfying than breaking those who had inherited great wealth and weren't smart, competent, or hardworking enough to hold onto it. He was especially disgusted by those who partied their lives and fortunes away. If they couldn't hold onto their wealth and position, they deserved to have it taken away.

There was a knock on his office door. "Come in."

"Good news," Phillip, his lawyer said as he came through the door. "The bank called in all loans this morning and foreclosed."

"Excellent," Pluta said with a satisfied smirk on his face.

"It gets better," Phillip said as he sat in the chair opposite Pluta's desk. "This afternoon he and his wife drank themselves nearly into a stupor. They left the bar, stumbled their way to the canyon bridge, and jumped off. There are two wet smears at the bottom of the ravine."

"Oh, how I would have loved to have seen that," said Pluta delighted. "So, the heir to the Cereo fortune will be out on the street soon."

Phillip hesitated, and looking a bit guilty said, "no, I imagine he'll stay at the villa until they run out of food, or taxes are due. The villa wasn't used as collateral in the last round of loans."

Pluta glared at Phillip said, "why didn't you get the villa?"

"I decided you would enjoy watching them try and be farmers on that worthless piece of property. Jenny was always bragging about how it was completely sustainable. This has been so much fun I was reluctant to see it end. How could I know they'd jump off a bridge. Jenny was the one who bought the property out in the middle of nowhere because she wanted to be closer to nature," he scoffed. "It just ended up being a place to park their kid while they gambled and partied."

"Well, she is close to nature now," Pluta joked. They both laughed. "So, what about the villa now?"

"The son just turned sixteen, which is the age of maturity in that backwards region. His slaves will likely kill him, steal everything, and run away. They certainly know there isn't anyone to inherit. Nobody will have an interest in chasing down a few slaves." Phillip explained. "We could argue his contract with us is vague enough to cover the villa and claim a debt equal to or greater than the value of the land, slaves, and livestock. As you know his idiot father signed a contract no one in their right mind would sign," he offered.

"Starving amidst pastoral beauty. Murdered by slaves. Almost poetic," Pluta said. "He'll fail on his own. Might provide some entertainment." Pluta considered his options, then he said smiling, "sign off on the debt and let probate go through. When he tries to borrow money or is late on taxes let me know." Pluta hesitated and said, "tell Henry to pull a case of the 10-year-old Gold Coast pinot noir out of the cellar and deliver it to your Domus.

"That's quite a gift sir," Phillip said with suspicion in his voice.

"Continue to deliver value and I'll continue to be generous," Pluta said smiling but with a tinge of threat the way he said 'continue to deliver value'.

"You know my weakness," laughed Phillip nervously.

Pluta just gave him a tight smile and dismissed him saying, "See you at the board meeting next week. Henry will see you out."

Pluta smiled at the memory of Phillip joking about Pluta's knowledge of his 'weakness'. His weakness wasn't wine. Not in the traditional way that alcohol was a weakness. But it was what triggered his downfall. His weakness was having a mother who was a common pleasure slave. His father had fallen in love with her and concocted an orphaned nephew story that had been accepted by the aristocracy. Pluta privately released this information. Phillip was blacklisted, debarred, and eventually bankrupt. The last bit was deliciously enjoyable. Phillip's sin? He had built a private wine cellar to hide his stock of Cereo's wines. Caius had initially built his fortune on wine and every wine snob on the planet had a collection of it. Pluta did not accept any hint of disloyalty from his employees or associates.

Coming back to the present, Pluta knew he had to find Caius Cereo's weakness. He must have at least one. As far as his sources could tell, Caius didn't bilk, bribe, or steal in his business dealings. He hadn't been caught cheating on his wife. He had never been accused of breaking any laws. Pluta had a lot of pride in his ability to hide his indiscretions. Caius was obviously a master at it as well. Pluta would not directly attack Caius's business interests. That was far too dangerous. Others had tried and failed. Some quite dramatically. He would have to wait, be patient. Everyone makes mistakes, and Caius would too. When he did, Pluta would relish finishing him and his entire family.

CHAPTER 14

# TRAJAN

Trajan, Fifth of his Name, was lounging in the central courtyard of the Palatium Trajan. The large garden was located in the center of the sprawling complex. The garden was a maze of walkways and seating areas surrounded by meticulously maintained ornamental vegetation. Numerous fountains added a pleasing background noise amidst the bright colors and fresh scents of flowering plants.

Trajan was stocky and had been ruggedly handsome in his youth. Now past middle age he was showing the effects of a life of excess. He was recovering from the previous night's activities and unhappy with the progress of his grand project. The year was Trajan 5-27, or the twenty seventh year of his reign. Other than the grand construction of Palatium Trajan, he felt he hadn't accomplished much as emperor of Arista. He fancied himself an equal of the roman emperors of antiquity. The grand accomplishment of the roman empire was conquest. His namesake had expanded the roman empire to its greatest extent. Trajan felt his destiny was to equal or exceed that accomplishment. It was taking too long.

Tajan looked up from his musings and saw Caius Cereo approaching with his ever-present valet walking a few steps behind him.

"Good morning cousin," Trajan said jovially. There were multiple messages in his now standard greeting. The first was a bit of a jab at the ever-present sycophants nearby. Caius was an actual distant relative. They had a common paternity that split off generations ago. He had started calling Caius his cousin when he first achieved visible power in the senate. He had noticed Magistrate Pluta visibly wincing the first time he jokingly did this in public. That cemented his use of the appellation. On the other hand, Trajan had publicly executed a number of his cousins after they had formulated a coup on his first anniversary as emperor. He had been young when his father died. His relatives had thought him weak. They had underestimated him. He knew it was a whispered joke that being related to Trajan was more dangerous than being his enemy. While not the most intelligent of emperors he was a cunning and vicious man. He knew it was important to keep the senate divided. Anything other than constant bickering and positioning for power between the senators was a threat. He privately preferred Caius over Pluta. He believed much of Caius's success was due to the superior blood line they shared. However, his primary goal was to keep the two of them at each other's throats.

"Good morning to you Trajan," Caius said smiling.

Caius had cleverly responded the first time he was addressed as cousin by simply calling him Trajan. He was unique in the senate by referring to Trajan as a family member would. Rather than being offended, Trajan had been amused. He appreciated a quick wit and bold moves. He felt the empire was suffering from a lack of risk taking and he valued the clever quick-thinking Caius. "The senatorial magistrate was here earlier and in a foul mood," Trajan said with a penetrating look.

"I can imagine he was upset with this morning's slave auction," Caius said with a conspiratorial smile.

Trajan then took on a more serious look and said accusingly, "you have upset plans Magistrate Pluta proposed to accelerate our conquest of Liberty."

Caius took on a determined look and said, "yes, I did that intentionally. Magistrate Pluta plans were inspired but not aggressive enough. Liberty should be a submissive region of the empire not a subject kingdom. The plan's flaws were a limitation on your control and a cap on eventual revenues.

You should accept nothing less than complete domination."

Trajan unknowingly reacted to Caius's use of the words submissive and domination. He had an unquenchable thirst for control. Watching others die at his whim was his ultimate satisfaction. The Arena satisfied some of this obsession. His punishment of criminals was akin to a sexual experience for Trajan. Nothing satisfied him more than having someone screaming in pain begging him to take their life. Trajan shook himself out of the fog he had been induced into and asked, "What are you going to do with the Pacifica gladiator?"

"I was planning on making him a New Years present," Caius said.

"Why not now? That was Pluta's offer," Trajan asked frowning.

"Turns out he's smaller than previous captives. While still impressive, it's not clear he's up to the standards set by previous Pacifica captives. If he performs well in the Arena on New Years then I'll give him to you. I didn't want to gift him now just to find out later he's mediocre. That would be an insult to you and an embarrassment for me," Caius said.

"You are always thinking cousin," Trajan said with a grin breaking out on his face. "There is no need to risk the reputation of my stable. We'll see how he stacks up." Trajan paused and affected a leer as he said, "I heard the queen's servant was uncommonly beautiful. That might have made an appropriate gift to compensate me for the change in plans."

"The queen and her servant are both part of the plan to conquer Liberty. If you are not supportive of my proposal, I will hand them both over to you. It will take some time to explain the intricacies of the new plan. Would it be possible to pull in your war planners and review?" Caius asked.

"Intriguing. As you saw on the way in there is a long line of people to see today. This short audience was to get an explanation of why you interfered this morning. I'll get an extended session scheduled." Trajan then affected a threatening tone saying, "I hope it's a good plan. Cousin or not, I won't be happy if you've slowed down Arista's conquest of Liberty."

"Understood Your Eminence," Caius said as he smiled, bowed low, and exited the courtyard.

CHAPTER 15

# THE GLADIATORS

As Tee was being led out of the auction house his concern was for Olivia and Gloria's safety. He had gotten to know both of them well during the weeks of travel. They were good hearted moral people. He would be happy to call them friends in better circumstances. His blood still boiled over the obscenely revealing dress they made Gloria wear. His anger had been further heightened by the comments he heard coming from that crowd of decadent bastards during her auction. He didn't know what would happen to the two women, but he swore an oath to find them if he ever escaped.

Queen Olivia had surprised him. The Pacifica history books had led him to believe royalty thought themselves better than others. Olivia didn't treat Gloria or himself that way at all. He was treated just like someone from home would treat him. He had to admit he was attracted to her. She was smart and witty. Although tiny by Pacifica standards, she had an athletic look he found appealing. What was really surprising was her knowledge of agriculture and animal husbandry. He didn't expect royalty to have that sort of working knowledge. In many ways it was like talking to someone from Apple Valley. Thoughts of home brought back thoughts of Diana. He had to move on from that fantasy, as difficult or impossible as that might be. He cautioned himself that life now simply revolved around staying alive. "Tee, you have a habit of being attracted to unobtainable women," he said out loud to himself shaking his head slowly in self-depreciating amusement.

They arrived at the Arena soon after leaving the auction house. It was an impressively large building with a number of smaller buildings enclosed within a high wall off to one side. It was to one of these buildings he was taken. He was placed in a cell much larger than the one he had on the slave ship. On board ship he only had a short narrow bed with a toilet and sink. This one had a large bed, a table with two chairs, bookcase, toilet, sink, and what appeared to be a large shower. Obscene luxury compared to his Guard accommodations. While all areas of his cell were open to viewing by the guards, the solid walls were arranged so that the other prisoners couldn't see into each other's cells. A barred window looked out into what appeared to be an exercise yard. It had shutters on the inside of the window. Privacy of a sort. On the slaver they had arranged a system where Olivia or Gloria would simply say "privacy please," and he would turn around until they said "done." It was embarrassing for everyone. He was glad he had some limited privacy.

Once he was locked in a cell, and his chains were removed, all but one of the contingent of guards left. The remaining guard was the oldest of the group and seemed to be in charge. He was a small thin man with grey hair and the look of someone who had lived a hard life. However, his eyes were bright with intelligence and Tee had noticed him carefully studying his new prisoner.

The old man looked him over once more and said blandly, "This is where you'll live until you die in the Arena or survive thirty matches. I've never seen a Pacifica gladiator win his freedom. The emperor tends to spread out matches for you folks and reserve them for special occasions. The good news is that you'll likely grow old here. You keep yourself and your cell clean, or we'll be forced to hose everything down. That gets everything wet which is uncomfortable. We'll bring you three meals a day. When you're done just slide the tray back out under the door. You'll get time in the training yard every day. This is for exercising and working on your fighting skills. Your owner will assign a handler. They are responsible for ensuring you're healthy and ready for the Arena. Your handler will likely want to see you demonstrate your skills this week so he knows what you can do. You are free to spar with the others if they agree to it. There will be blunt weapons and the like for that. If you seriously injure a guard or another gladiator your exercise privileges will be revoked. The Arena is the only place you are allowed to seriously injure anyone." He stopped talking for a moment, looked Tee in the eyes and said in a more friendly and slightly pleading voice, "you are from Pacifica. I'm sure if you decided to kill me it wouldn't take much effort on your part. The guards aren't your enemy. We are slaves just like you. Our lives depend on doing what we're told. If you kill one of us you won't be killing an enemy."

Tee was touched by this revelation. He had been looking for ways to get at the guards. Knowing they were slaves changed his opinion of them. They weren't his captors; they were fellow captives. He looked the guard in the eye and said, "in Pacifica slavery is outlawed. We believe it's a crime against God. Only God has dominion over humankind. Don't worry about me. I understand your situation and don't resent you for the actions of others. I have no reason to harm you." While Tee couldn't trust the guards to go against their own self-interest, they were potential allies. He would treat them with kindness and respect.

The guard looked visibly relieved and said, "my name is Dobler. If you cooperate I'll do what I can to make your life as pleasant as is possible in this place."

"Thank you Dobler. You can call me Tee." And with that Dobler turned and walked off down the hall.

The next morning after breakfast Dobler showed up. "You have the morning shift in the exercise yard today. There will be a number of other gladiators there and they might challenge you to spar. Like I said yesterday please don't kill or seriously injure anyone. It would be really boring sitting in your cell all day every day." Then he opened Tee's cell and motioned him out.

"Aren't you going to chain me?" Tee asked.

"No, I have a feeling you're a decent human being. If you kill me I'll go to my maker knowing I've had a better life than most," Dobler said seriously. Then he hesitated and smiling said, "and the knowledge that I'm not as good a judge of character as I think I am."

Tee smiled, he liked Dobler. Deciding to be honest he said, "I'm not planning to live the rest of my life here. But I won't kill innocent people in exchange for my freedom."

"Fair enough. Can't hold it against you if you try to escape. Just so you know, we've never had anyone succeed," Dobler said conversationally. Then with a grin he said, "I would appreciate you not escaping on my shift."

Tee grinned and replied, "I won't promise, but I'll keep it in mind."

Walking down the hallway they passed cell after cell of small but rough looking men. They were quiet and studying him intently. They were clearly measuring their chances against him. One of them finally asked Dobler, "Is he from Pacifica?"

"Newly arrived," Dobler replied.

They soon stood in front of a short corridor leading to the exercise yard. The corridor had locked gates on each end. Dobler opened the first gate and motioned him into the corridor. As he locked the gate behind Tee he said, "at noon we switch to another group. You have six hours if you want them. Call out to the guards in the observation booth if you want to go back early." Then he motioned Tee to walk to the gate on the far end where a new guard stood waiting for him. This guard was young and looked nervous. He hesitated then said in a questioning voice that quavered a bit, "my name is Eric. Dobler says you won't kill me if I open this gate."

"I have no reason to harm you," Tee said in a soft reassuring voice.

Eric unlocked the gate, backed away, and quickly disappeared through a doorway to his right. Tee entered the courtyard and looked around. Above and behind him was a large balcony with heavy bars protecting the observing occupants. As he scanned the men and women watching him Eric emerged and gave him a nervous wave.

There was an oval running track alongside the walls of the large rectangular courtyard. In the middle was a round ring that looked like a place to spar. Spread across the rest of the open area were weights and various devices. Some he was familiar with; some he was not. There was an archery and spear range with a high and wide wooden barrier up against the inside of the track at one end to protect the runners. It had been over a month since he had gone for a run, so he started with that.

The lower gravity made it easier, but a month without a hard run eventually earned him a burning sensation in his side. While he was running around the track he noticed a large older man with a long-braided ponytail watching him. He was certainly large enough to be from Pacifica. But no one from home would disgrace themselves by wearing their hair in that fashion. After an hour he stopped running. His breathing was even but he was having to breath deeper than he normally would. It would take a few days, but he would get back into shape. Next he worked hard with the weights and went through his entire regiment of Guard exercises. Six days on, one day off was the mantra and he would stick to it. It felt good to be out of confinement. Then he realized his cage was simply a bit larger.

Just before the change in shifts a voice called out from the observation deck, "challenge him."

One of the larger gladiators approached him and asked, "would you like to spar? No weapons just hand to hand."

Tee considered this and then agreed, "Ok, what are the rules?"

"Bruises are ok but nothing serious. If either of us says Halt, that ends the match."

Tee nodded his head then the man said, "are you really

from Pacifica? You're not as big as the other one."

"Yes, I'm from Pacifica," Tee said forcefully, tension in his voice. He was angry. The older man was obviously 'the other one' and was parading around with braided hair. Nobody from the Guard would do that. It was even more insulting for a common citizen to affect it.

His opponent backed away a step until Tee waved him forward and they began. Tee's opponent said, "Halt," after being knocked to the ground for the fifth time without landing a blow. Two others challenged and just as quickly ended their engagements with him. Tee was actually drawing the matches out, not showing his true skills. The Guard had taught him to do that. He would only show enough to win and no more.

After the third sparring match Dobler was there to let him back into the gladiator's residence hall. Tee looked up before re-entering the corridor and studied the man who had directed the other gladiators to challenge him. They locked eyes and the man nodded.

"Who was the man with Eric in the observation room," Tee asked.

"That's your handler," Dobler said. "Would you like to meet him?"

"Do I have a choice?" Tee asked.

"You do. But it's to your advantage to get to know him. Like me, he's a slave and the only friend you'll have in this place. You'll never get close to your owner, or any citizen for that matter."

"Ok, how and when?" Tee inquired.

"Now and in your cell. The reason there are two chairs with your table is that you can have visitors. We lock you in, but you can have guests. Most of the gladiators avoid each other except to train. You never know who you're going to have to kill later," Dobler said with a sad tone in his voice.

"How about you? Can you visit me in my cell," Tee

asked.

"I'm your keeper. I'm not someone you should trust. I have to report on everything you say and do. But yes, we can share a few stories in the evening if you like." Dobler hesitated a moment and then said with a friendly grin, "I'll add honesty to your list of attributes."

"Why do you say that?" Tee asked.

"Last night you told me you wouldn't kill innocents for your freedom. Today you told Eric you had no reason to harm him. You never promised either one of us safety. Most will lie when we ask them and give an empty promise." Dobler paused then said, "honesty is measured here by only lying when you have to."

Tee smiled at that description. He had to admit he wasn't the most honest person he knew, that was Quinn's domain. His personal rule for honesty was not to lie about something that would benefit himself unfairly or harm another person. He wasn't perfect. But he was very disappointed in himself when he failed. The rule had to be different in this situation. He liked Dobler's definition and decided to adopt it until he escaped this nightmare.

The man he had seen in the observation room walked up with Dobler and introduced himself, "my name is Leo. My master decided I'm to be your handler. It's less controlling than it sounds. I'm to ensure you are getting what you need to be your best in the Arena. From what I saw today you don't need any help from me on training. I can also take requests back to our master for you."

Tee studied the man for a few moments before responding. Leo was heavy set but shorter than Dobler, who Tee had decided was of normal height based on his observations so far. He had dark hair and a coppery complexion with green eyes. Tee then turned to Dobler and said, "let him in. He'll be safe."

Leo sat down at Tee's table and said, "let me start by explaining who I am and a little about our master. I'm our master's personal valet. That means I am constantly at his side providing services. As a consequence, you won't see me often. I was born on our master's estate as a slave. I will be a slave for the rest of my life. Our master never frees slaves. He says it's for our own good." This last bit was said with a hint of a smirk.

"Thank you for being honest with me and not giving me false hope. I will return that honesty by telling you that no man is my master," Tee said firmly.

Leo smiled at that and said, "I respect your beliefs Tee. But you need to accept your reality. I will help you as much as I can. But there is nothing you can do to gain your freedom."

Tee nodded grimly. They had an understanding; he didn't like it, but at least Leo seemed to be a decent person. Broken, but decent.

Leo nodded back at him and said, "I'm not sure when I'll be back so let me tell you what I know about your immediate future. Your first visit to the Arena will be in four months at the Harvest Celebration. That is a yearly national holiday to give thanks for the blessings Arista has bestowed on us. I don't know who or what you'll face. It might be some of the other gladiators here or it might be criminals or captives of some sort. Likely it will be more than one at the same time. Assuming you survive that, you'll definitely be included in the New Years celebration. This is the biggest and most elaborate event of the year at the Arena."

Tee accepted this news and then leaned forward. "What can you tell me of Olivia and Gloria? I know your master purchased them as well."

Leo sat back and considered this. Then he said. "I have met them both and they are well. It would have been far worse for both of them had the other bidder won. Before you ask, I won't take any messages to them." He said this last bit firmly.

"Thank you. If you change your mind, tell them I'll be

coming for them," Tee said with ice in his eyes.

This visibly surprised Leo. After a pause he seemed to be delighted by it as well. "I might actually do that," he said and chuckled. "Let Dobler know if you need anything from me. He can always get in touch." Still smiling slightly with his gaze remaining on Tee he called out, "Dobler, I'm ready to go." Dobler came quickly, he must have been just around the corner.

"See, I told you he wouldn't tear you into a hundred pieces," Dobler said in an amused tone unlocking his cell. They both disappeared down the hallway.

The next two days were much like the first in the recreation yard. The only exception is that Tee could tell his wind was returning. As before, gladiators would challenge near the end of their allotted time, and he would quickly defeat them. On the third day the other Pacifica gladiator was in the yard, continuing to watch him. When he was done with his run he limped over to Tee and said, "you want to spar?"

Tee looked daggers at him barely able to keep his anger in check. He bit off a quick, "yes." Then he settled in to punish this pretender for his insult. Tee feigned to his right intending to unbalance the big man by putting his weight on what was obviously a bad leg. He was aiming to grab his braid and yank him to the ground. The next thing he knew he was on his back seeing stars.

"That was pathetic," the old man said with disgust on his face. "Get up and try again."

Tee got up and decided to be a bit more cautious this time. A different result this time. Now he was face down in the dirt. He tried a more defensive approach for the next round. Other than bruises in new places it wasn't any different. After a few more rounds Tee was covered in dirt which his sweat was turning to mud. His opponent was untouched, unsoiled, and seemingly accomplishing this with little to no effort.

"Who are you?" Tee finally asked.

"My name is Victor. Are you actually in the Guard?" he said with anger in his voice.

"Yes, first year Newbie. Are you really Vic?" Tee asked.

"Only my friends call me that. You call me Victor," he said sternly. Then turning his head towards the sky he said, "God, what has happened to my Guard!" Turning back to glare at Tee he seemed to consider what to say for a few moments and then said "Tell Dobler yes when he asks if you'll accept me as a guest tonight. We have things to discuss." He then turned around and walked off. Instead of the uncoordinated limping and stooped posture that had been affected since Tee arrived, Victor walked like a panther, smooth, graceful, and radiating danger.

Tee couldn't have been more embarrassed. Even walking away Victor was insulting him for being so stupid as to underestimate an opponent, buying into false deficiencies. The man wasn't insulting the memory of Vic, he was Vic! In the lore of the Guard there wasn't a more godlike figure. In recruit training they make you shave your head the first time you lose a bout. The instructors made sure this happened during their initial physical fitness assessment. Your hair stayed shaved for the rest of your life in the Guard. The idea being that you shouldn't have hair long enough for an opponent to grab. Victor never shaved his. As a recruit he never lost a bout. Even the instructors couldn't best him. Victor was a nickname from his recruitment days when every bout declared him 'The Victor'.

How could this be? Tee asked himself. Victor disappeared before he was born. The story was that he went out on a scouting mission and never returned. But it must be him Tee thought. While he wasn't the best hand-to-hand fighter he always managed to get in a strike here and there. Even when sparring with Jay. He never got close to that with Victor. "Well, it ought to be interesting to hear what he has to say," Tee said aloud to himself.

Later that evening, Victor didn't waste any time on pleasantries. "If you are what's in the Guard now something horrible has happened. Tell me what's happened since I was captured."

That set Tee back a bit, but he could understand Victor's conclusion given Tee's unconventional path to the Guard. Tee proceeded to update Victor on news and battles with the GEMs since his disappearance. When he got to the one he had participated in he slowed down and gave a detailed description for every day of the battle. He kept it general and didn't mention his role or activities.

"Setting the moat on fire and marching out with a Phalanx was clever. I would have liked to have seen that. We never had a chance to try the Phalanx out. It was always intended to be a last-ditch surprise to cover a retreat to the dam."

"Who is master sergeant now?" Victor asked.

"Griffith Risk," Tee answered.

"No shit. Griff's still alive? That warms an old man's heart. Is he still grumpy?" Victor asked, again with the corners of his mouth slightly upturned.

"Yes, very," Tee said trying a smile back.

The conversation progressed through old Guard members still around who Victor knew. Victor's interest peaked when he mentioned his mother was a Wall Archer. "What's her name?" asked Victor.

"Arti Stone," Tee answered.

"Maiden name Green?" Victor asked with interest.

"Yes," Tee answered.

"Your mother is little Arti Green?" Victor asked incredulously, and then said nostalgically. "She was an arrow monkey the last time I saw her. I remember her because she was wicked with a bow. Already better than most of the experienced Wall Archers. They all talked about her. God that makes me feel old." He hesitated, looked Tee over anew and then said, "that explains why you pay attention to the archers." Victor stopped thoughtfully and looked Tee in the eye and asked in a low voice. "How good are you? No false modesty."

Tee hesitated; he had been avoiding the archery range hiding that skill. This was Victor however and if he wanted to know Tee would give him an honest answer. "My mother is the only one who can best me."

"And how good is she?" Victor asked.

"She's won the archery competition in every Game held since she reached maturity," Tee said in a low voice brimming with pride.

"I should have guessed." Victor said berating himself. "It's obvious. The callus patterns on your hands and the uneven musculature. Have seen the same thing on some of the better Wall Archers. Can't believe I didn't put it together." He stopped for a few moments to consider what he had just learned. "Continue to keep it a secret. You should practice. Don't do it very often or they will get suspicious. Just enough to stay sharp. Aim at something different every time and convince everyone you're worthless at it. Show frustration. We can't afford to ignore something that might give us an advantage."

Victor stopped then and asked, "who invited you to recruit training?"

"Griff," Tee answered.

This clearly surprised Victor. He paused for a while looking at Tee with more interest. "Are you related to him?" he asked suspiciously.

"No, the Guard doesn't allow that sort of thing," Tee answered looking back defiantly, more than a little insulted.

"Thank God that hasn't changed. Ok, I'm missing something." Victor paused to think it through. After a while he said. "Griff used to say the Guard needed to be more than a bunch of brutes bashing about. What else can you do besides archery."

Tee sighed deeply, turned red embarrassed by the question. Then he said, "Griff told me he wanted me in the Guard because I'm good at coming up with unconventional battle plans."

Victor just looked at him in confusion for a few moments and then asked, "can you give me an example?"

"Lighting the moat and driving the GEMs into it with a Phalanx was my suggestion," Tee said with his face turning even redder.

"I'll be damned," Victor said clearly delighted. "Griff has you earmarked to be an officer doesn't he? If that idea is an example of your contributions maybe he was right all along. We all used to make fun of him for saying that." Victor stopped and stared at Tee for a few moments making him uncomfortable.

"There is no excuse for your incompetence in the ring," he said as his eyes bored into him. "They trained you for defensive fighting. It's better than your laughable offensive skills but it's far short of acceptable. I've lived here longer than I lived on Pacifica. Someone is going to pay for that, and I want you to help me. To do that you have to be turned into a competent fighter. You want to help me make them pay?"

"Nothing would make me happier," Tee said honestly.

"Good, then reserve three hours every day in the yard for practice. We are also going to have dinner together whenever I have something to discuss with you. You'll do exactly what I tell you to do. We'll have to start your training from scratch so plan on being frustrated and angry most of the time. No sparring with the other gladiators. It will just give you bad habits and you have enough of those already." Victor said sternly. Then softening his tone he added, "some advice. Don't talk to the other gladiators. They are used to my aloofness and will figure it's a Pacifica thing. You are likely going to have to kill many of them in the arena. It makes it easier if you don't know anything about their personal lives."

And with that he yelled, "Dobler we're done."

The next day Tee asked Eric. "Can I get a bow and some practice arrows?"

"I thought archery was a women's thing on Pacifica?" Eric asked confused.

"It is, but I'm bored. It will give me something new to do," Tee replied. Then he thought to himself, it will also give me something to be secretly good at while Victor humiliates me in front of everyone.

CHAPTER 16

# ARCHERS AUXILIARY

It had taken several long frustrating sessions, but the CGG finally agreed. Ultimately it was two of Griff's staff sergeants who convinced him. The CGG decided to bring them in to ask questions given how often Griff kept referring to them in his arguments. Their enthusiasm surprised him. It wasn't that the CGG didn't believe Griff. It was that he didn't think the rank and file would accept this kind of change. The Guard's self-identity was very strong. Sergeants Willis and Glenn had strong opinions about the excellence of Apple Valley Wall archers. They were convinced the group was much better than the other two regions. When asked if they would support a few Wall Archers becoming a permanent part of the Guard they enthusiastically supported it.

As Sergeant Willis put it, "Arti Stone is the reason the Apple Valley Wall Archers are so effective. Just having her spend full time training across all the regions would enhance effectiveness. If we coordinated training with the Guard I think the improvement would be tremendous."

Sergeant Glenn chimed in as well, "our scout teams would be greatly enhanced by some of their better archers. Diana Wells and her small team decimated the GEMs guarding the rope ladders during the upper east valley invasion. It saved lives and was the reason for our quick victory. Just one or two archers per scout team would make a difference."

After the two Scout Team leaders left the CGG said, "Ok

Griff I'm sold. Let's pull together a proposal for President Malrey. I would like to start small and see how it goes before commissioning a full-blown organization. Perhaps two archers from each of the regions. I believe the proposal hinges on Arti Stone agreeing to lead this. We need a name for the group. The Guard and its traditions are something specific. I don't want that to change. The Wall Archers aren't going to go through recruit training and other Guard type processes, so we don't need to muddy the water by trying to completely combine them. Perhaps we should ask Arti to figure all this out."

One week later President Malrey brought the Council back to order, "I believe we're ready for the last item on our agenda. This is a proposal I'm asking the Council to vote on even though it is within my authority to decide. I'll hand over the floor to the CGG to explain."

"Good afternoon. In our most recent struggles with the GEMs, it's become clear to the Guard how vital Wall Archers are to overall success. It's also become clear that the training Apple Valley has been doing has greatly increased their effectiveness in battle." The CGG paused, looked at Councilwoman Ricks, and gave a slight smile and nod of appreciation knowing her history. "It's common knowledge that Arti Stone is responsible. Our proposal is that we fund a permanent unit of Wall Archers that is separate from but under the command structure of the Guard. By having full-time focus, and the ability to jointly train, we believe we can significantly improve our defensive capabilities. We would like funding approval for six full-time Wall Archers, two from each region. Arti Stone would be asked to lead this unit. Questions?"

Councilwoman Ricks spoke up, "what if Arti says no."

"Then we drop the idea. We believe Arti could eventually train a replacement for herself but to start this up it will take her unique knowledge, skills, and reputation among the Wall Archer community."

"Great answer. I fully agree," Ricks said with a smile.

Barlow jumped in and said, "I don't think we ought to approve anything for the military until we agree to make a serious attempt at peace negotiations. After seeing thousands of dead from the latest battle they might be more inclined to stop this madness."

"You are well within your rights to call for an agenda item to discuss peace negotiations Councilman Barlow. But I recommend we not tie agenda items together. It will likely impede progress," President Malrey cautioned.

"I have a vote and will cast it anyway I like Ms. President," he said with a sneer.

Jennifer just stared at him for a moment collecting herself. Barlow had progressively gotten more and more combative in the past few months. He seemed to think she was the problem when she was simply a facilitator for the Pacifica Council. She had hoped bringing a decision to the council that was wholly hers to make would be an olive branch. It appeared that collaborative gestures weren't going to make things better.

"If there are no more questions or comments I move we vote," Jennifer said stiffly and waited. After a few moments of silence, she started.

"Councilwoman Ricks?"

"I vote yea. Arti is a national treasure, and this will make us safer."

Councilman Rickets?

"I vote nay. Barlow is right. We are too militaristic. Death and destruction seems to be our answer for everything. I for one am sick of it."

Jennifer was shocked. Looking quickly over at Councilwoman Ricks she could read the surprise on her face as well. She knew Rickets had lost a son at the Wall. Perhaps he was angry about that. She could certainly emphasize having just lost a younger brother during the last day of battle. Losing the full support of Apple Valley was extremely disturbing from a number of perspectives.

The rest of the voting was quick and predictable. Landing Valley voting yea and Eureka Valley voting nay.

Jennifer looked around the room and after catching everyone's eye said, "I brought this issue to the council to test the appetite for military spending. I can see we need to restart discussions on how to approach the GEMs with peace proposals. We lost a good portion of our Guard and Volunteer forces at the Wall in the most recent battle. Given the situation I don't believe we can wait on proposals that potentially increase our effectiveness. For that reason, I will break the tie with a yea vote."

"Councilman Rickets. Given your strong stance on it will you come back with a proposal for peace negotiations? Feel free to work with any of your fellow councilpersons."

"I appreciate the offer Ms. President. Can I have two weeks to prepare?"

"Yes. I'll add it to the agenda two weeks from today. This Pacifica Council session is now completed."

Griff's visit to Apple Valley wasn't going as expected. It was confusing to say the least. He had expected Arti to be as warm and friendly as she had been lately. She was not. Her treatment of him had been coldly professional. This wasn't the Arti he had come to know. After explaining the Wall Archer leadership role that was being offered she had a few questions.

"How often will I be working directly with the Guard?" Arti asked.

Griff hesitated a moment still confused by her seemingly angry disposition. Then he said, "that is something you will propose. You know how the Guard operates at the Wall. I think you're in the best position to decide what is most efficient. I would like to discuss how archers can be deployed alongside our Scout teams. Diana's success at the upper east valley incursion has sparked a lot of ideas to improve those teams' effectiveness as well."

"How often will I have to work with you?" she asked

pointedly with ice in her eyes.

"As much or as little as you think necessary," he said. His heart was in his throat as he wondered what he had done to make her this angry.

Just then the door to Arti's house opened and Grammy strolled in. She didn't seem any happier than Arti. Without so much as a hello Grammy said with iron in her voice, "I heard you were here. You know something about Tee's disappearance. I want to know what you know."

"What makes you think I know something," Griff replied.

Grammy huffed out a big breath, composed herself and said. "Diana is like a granddaughter to me. At times I know her better than she knows herself. She has been cagy about what was found over on the east side. That isn't like her. She's also acting like Tee isn't dead. She hasn't said anything to anyone, but I know that girl. I also know that if she knows something, you know something."

"If you think Diana knows something, ask her," Griff replied with his voice becoming stern.

"I have, and she lies to me," Grammy said. "You must have scared her into keeping what happened to Tee a secret."

"I have not threatened Diana. I'm also not going to lie so don't ask me anything else about this," Griff said in a loud voice.

"I think you should leave now. I will accept the position offered but I would appreciate keeping our interactions to a minimum," Arti said in a raised but quavering voice.

Griff just stared at her for a moment, his heart going out to her. Then he said, "I'll assign Jay Phillips as your primary Guard contact. He is working for me as an aide and most of what needs to happen can happen through him. And before you ask, Jay doesn't know anything about Tee's disappearance." He hesitated for a few moments and said, "One more thing. They found Angus Willard hanging from a tree in a remote area of the Armstrong Reservoir. The Landfall Valley Sheriff isn't investigating, and neither is the

Guard." After delivering that news Griff opened the door and left. He was heartsick. Tears threatening to form in his eyes. But he would honor his oath to keep everything about the Committee secret. His personal desires were insignificant compared to the safety and security of Pacifica.

CHAPTER 17

# CAIUS

Senator Cereo was in the entry hall to personally greet him when the First Minister arrived. They walked a short distance down the hall and into a small but warm office. "Thank you for making the time to meet with me Senator," Jack said with a polite smile.

"Good to see you again Jack. I enjoyed our conversation at my little party. Thank you again for taking the time to attend." He hesitated a moment and then continued, "I'm not much on formalities so please just call me Caius."

Jack was struck once again by the senator's easy-going nature. He didn't have the upper-class snobbery common among the colonist elite. Perhaps it was his rural upbringing. However, Jack had seen glimpses of steel in his nature at the senator's party so he would proceed cautiously. "I have some delicate topics to discuss. Is it possible to have some privacy?" he asked glancing over at a slave sitting in a corner of the room.

"You can discuss anything you want in front of Leo. He's my valet and you can trust him to keep his mouth shut. He's not stupid enough to cross me. Nor is he smart enough to take advantage of anything you say," Caius said disdainfully.

Jack had heard the senator was unusually paranoid about his safety. Evidently several assassination attempts had been made over the years. One recent attempt was reported to have been made by a highly regarded and expensive professional. That man had gotten into Caius's private suite at his remote villa. But he only killed one elderly servant before being killed himself. Jack studied the senator's valet. He was heavily set and with his buzz cut he looked more like an army sergeant than a house servant. Jack was sure this was part of his personal security so unlikely to be a threat.

"I wanted to discuss one of your recent acquisitions at the slave market," Jack said.

Caius looked at him, smiled and said "You can be blunt with me Jack. Outside of the games that must be played at parties, I prefer to speak plainly. You strike me as an intelligent person. I'm sure you have specific things you'd like out of our conversation. Feel free to dive in."

He couldn't let it affect his decision making; but he couldn't help but like the senator. Jack gave Caius a conspiratorial grin and said, "that will certainly save us time and eliminate confusion." When Caius nodded back at him he continued, "you have possession of Queen Olivia. Magistrate Pluta had plans for her he claimed would increase tax revenues for the Commonwealth. We would like to know what you have planned for her."

"Is the Commonwealth going to ask if she can be released to Magistrate Pluta?" Caius asked.

"No, certainly not. As you know we can't legally compel you to do that," Jack said, emphasizing the word legally in a way that insinuated this wasn't really a barrier. "The Commonwealth is always interested in supporting colonists within the boundaries of the Edicts."

Caius gave a warm smile and said, "my initial objective was to be a pain in the ass. As you know Jack, Pluta and I are business and political competitors. I didn't know at the time what he had planned for her but wanted to ensure it didn't create a problem for me."

"That makes sense. But, again, what do you have planned?" Jack asked.

"I was originally thinking I would ransom her. It would fill my coffers and keep her away from Pluta. However, after studying the situation in Liberty I've concluded a bigger play might be possible," Caius said. "I'm not being evasive Jack. I still haven't come up with a plan that doesn't have significant issues. But I'm working on it."

"Is it something the Commonwealth could help with?" offered Jack

"Perhaps," Caius said thoughtfully. "Can I share some thoughts and have them stay private?"

"I have to report all conversations with colonists to the governor. But I am authorized to commit on her behalf that she will keep anything you say in confidence. The Administration function is not obligated to share information we obtain from planetary governments or colonists with Judicial. Unless of course something violating Commonwealth Edicts is proposed or exposed," Jack said in a tone that insinuated one again that legality was a negotiable topic.

Caius tapped his finger lightly on the table as he considered Jacks conditions. Looking Jack in the eye he said, "I'm intrigued by the possibility of conquering Liberty and putting the population to work. The emperor has long had a desire to conquer that planet. But, he doesn't have a plan to accomplish it without taking on an unacceptable level of risk. Worse yet, he doesn't have a plan of what to do if he's successful. Their army is smaller than ours. But long supply lines and decades of war producing excellent military leadership in Liberty steers me away from the direct approach. So, it has to start with a political solution, and we have their queen."

"How about forcing a state marriage between the queen and a member of the emperor's family. Over time you could take control," Jack said voicing the plan he had with Pluta. "Once you have control you change their constitution to allow slavery and start with the regions that have recently rebelled."

Caius appeared to be considering this carefully before saying. "In my opinion that isn't good enough. There are too many things that can go wrong. We have to eliminate Prince Justin and neutralize General Eastbrook for starters. Once that's done we have to eliminate the queen's power without it looking like a coup. Assuming we accomplish all that the House of Lords would have a say in the succession since a prince consort from Arista would likely be deemed a foreign national and not qualified." Caius hesitated a moment and then said, "we need to conquer them. Their constitution needs to be torn up. Trying to work within their system is unlikely to work and even if it did it would limit profits. We have to divide their kingdom and then conquer it. But it has to be done very carefully."

Jack had to think about that for a minute. Trying to buy time he asked, "What is your interest in this?"

"I would like to be the emperor's governor of Liberty once it's conquered. I would sign a tax revenue agreement with the Commonwealth in exchange for its assistance. My compensation would be based on a percentage of the increased taxes that are collected."

Jack nodded his head acknowledging his understanding. He wondered if Caius had grander goals in mind, perhaps as ruler of an independent Liberty? Needing more time to consider this change in plans he said, "I'm sure the governor would be interested in your thoughts on a tax revenue contract. Let me discuss it with her and get back to you."

"While you're doing that I'm going to fix the mess Pluta created. Liberty will naturally blame Arista for the queens kidnapping. This weakens any plans the emperor might have had by unifying Liberty rather than dividing it. I have a message to Prince Justin and the House of Lords ready for the emperor's seal. It exposes a plot by unknown parties in Liberty who bribed the slavers to capture the queen and transport her for sale to Arista," Caius explained.

Jack brow wrinkled and he said, "Doesn't that mean you'll have to hand her over to Liberty and lose our leverage?"

"No. In his message the emperor will express paternal concern for the queen's well-being. He'll state that he doesn't know who paid to have her kidnapped. Given that, he has no idea who he can safely release her to," Caius said smiling. "He'll go on to say that he is very interested in working with the kingdom of Liberty to expose whoever is trying to create problems between their two worlds."

Jack was clearly still not convinced and said, "given that message, won't Queen Olivia just decide to return to Liberty?"

"It will be pointed out that Queen Olivia has not reached the age of maturity according to Arista law. The emperor will state that he is so concerned for her safety that he personally designated one of Arista's leading citizens as guardian. He states in the message that his only goal is to ensure long lasting peace with Liberty," Caius said with his winning smile. "It turns out I'm a hero of the empire by recognizing Queen Olivia and quickly taking control of her safety. As a show of good faith, the servant who was taken along with her will be immediately released. She has been well treated since leaving the auction house and her account of time spent on Arista will align with the emperor's message." Caius hesitated then and with a smug expression said. "This did present a personal challenge. Her servant was unusually attractive. I was very tempted to keep her. However, the needs of Arista and the Commonwealth come first."

Jack was very impressed. He wasn't sure what the next steps were, but Caius's plan kept them in control of the queen while causing strife and confusion in Liberty. Jack considered everything and then asked, "is there anything you need from the Commonwealth in the short term?"

"It would be helpful if the Commonwealth didn't refute the claim that someone on Liberty paid for the queen's transportation to Arista. By declining to confirm or deny Liberty based involvement, the natural assumption will be that the Commonwealth confirms the accusation." Caius hesitated, then he said with a knowing look, "I believe

Magistrate Pluta has been ignoring messages from Lord Druango."

At this point Jack wasn't surprised Caius knew their plans. His ability to take control meant his sources of inside information were excellent. "Yes, he doesn't know what to tell Druango, so he's been buying time."

"You might let Lord Druango know privately that the rumor on Arista is that Prince Justin is the culprit. That he's trying to supplant the queen now that her father is gone. Expressing concern for Druango's health at the same time might be a nice touch," Caius suggested. He let that sink in for a few moments and then continued, "in addition, it would be ideal if General Eastbrook's surveillance network intercepted a message indicating Lord Druango provided the slavers bribe. His plan was to convict Prince Justin on a second count of treason, execute him, and then negotiate with Arista to get the queen returned. The nice touch here is to have plans to eliminate Justin's and General Eastbrook's extended families as part of the intercepted message. The conspiracy clearly intends to isolate the queen and leave her as the only living member of the royal line."

Jack's head was spinning. This was much more aggressive, and devious, than their original plan. The financial windfall would be enormous if they pulled it off. But it would mean another delay. He wasn't looking forward to delivering a schedule change to the governor. On the other hand, she might be intrigued by Senator Cereo's plan. The confusion he was going to sow didn't present a problem for the Commonwealth. Another civil war was obviously Caius's goal here and there was only upside to that outcome. He would have to come up with an alternative plan for the governor to consider. Just going in with Caius's plan would make him look weak.

"Thanks again for seeing me. I'll be in touch once I've discussed this with the Governor. I'm looking forward to seeing what we can accomplish together," Jack said.

Caius walked him all the way out to his carriage asking

about his family and how he was enjoying his new role as First Minister. It was a nice touch. Most powerful people hand that duty off to a servant and wouldn't bother to ask personal questions. As his carriage drove off he realized with alarm that he liked the senator. The extent of the man's deviousness made him extremely wary, but he was oddly likeable. He counseled himself that having personal regard for anyone was dangerous. You never knew when they would need to be sacrificed.

CHAPTER 18

# SALT THE EARTH

The messenger arrived late in the afternoon through driving rain. The Lieutenant was wet, grimy, exhausted, and escorted by a small contingent of rangers. The roads had gotten dangerous since the queen's kidnapping. Criminal elements were taking advantage of the military prioritizing preparations for renewed civil war rather than chasing down criminals. They hadn't gotten so bold as to attack a military unit yet, but safety on the roads was getting worse every day.

When he was ushered into the ranch house Perry was having a late dinner with Olivia, Colonel Peters, and a few of his staff officers. The rangy young man hesitated at the door clearly intimated by those seated at the table. Perry recognizing his hesitancy rose and warmly greeted him, "come sit and have dinner with us. Lieutenant Graves? Is that right?" he asked.

"Yes sir," Graves answered, clearly surprised Perry knew his name.

Turning to one of the two soldiers serving them he asked, "would you get another place setting and some hot tea for the Lieutenant? I'm sure he's chilled to the bone."

"Thank you sir but I don't want to impose," Graves said clearly uncomfortable dining with the top Army officers.

Perry noticed Graves self-consciously looking down at his mud splattered uniform and remembered his own days as a young lieutenant. "Please join us. You can give your report and get a decent meal at the same time. What kind of soldier turns down a meal or a chance to sleep?" Perry said conveying his origins as an ordinary soldier.

"A stupid one sir," Graves answered with a shy smile quoting the axiom learned in basic training .

Perry had noticed the look Graves had given Olivia when the introductions were made. If his memory served him he had seen the young man on duty at the castle before the kidnapping. He had likely seen both Olivia and Bria up close. His wide-eyed glance at Olivia had given him away. His shocked look betrayed that he knew this was not Bria. Oh well, he thought, another soldier to add to the list of those not allowed to leave the ranch.

"I can see that you recognized the queen lieutenant," Perry said in a serious tone.

"Yes sir," Graves said nervously. Then turning to Olivia, he bowed low and said, "my apologies for not addressing you correctly Your Majesty."

Olivia smiled warmly and said, "please sit down and have dinner with us Lieutenant. You were right to play along with our little secret. I would appreciate it if you would refer to me as Bria for the time being. At some point we can get back to Your Majesty, or ma'am depending on the circumstances. For now, it's vital we continue the pretense that I'm the General's daughter."

"What do we do when an enemy makes a mistake Lieutenant?" Perry asked with a tight grin.

"We don't correct them sir," Graves answered smiling. Clearly becoming more comfortable.

"Good man," Perry said. "Please eat your dinner and then we can review your message packet and verbal report." Perry was pleased to see the young man attack his dinner with gusto. His guess was that the man hadn't stopped to eat anything since he left the castle. That told him much about the importance of the information he would deliver.

When Lieutenant Graves folded up his napkin and placed

it on his plate Perry said, "give us your report including what is in your packet. I'm also interested in any thoughts or impressions you have on moral among the troops given all the strife." He then looked around the table and said, "we'll wait until you're finished before we ask questions."

Graves took a deep breath and gave his report. "In the packet is a copy of a message from Emperor Trajan of Arista. The summary is that he claims shock and anger at the kidnapping of the queen and strongly states his dedication to finding those responsible. He goes on to say that his belief is that someone from Liberty is responsible. He says he will protect the queen's safety until the guilty parties are identified and neutralized. Since he doesn't know who to trust, and the queen is considered a minor under their laws, he will take on a paternal role and keep her safe on Arista." Graves paused at that point given everyone was leaning over the table clearly wanting to ask questions.

"Please continue Lieutenant," Perry said calmly but greatly relieved to have news of his daughter's whereabouts and situation. Perhaps he could even get a good night's sleep tonight.

Graves nodded his head and resumed his report. "Also in the packet are three messages from Prince Justin. The first details the latest developments in the House of Lords along with rumors the prince thinks may be legitimate. The second and third are written in code and for your eyes only," Graves said looking at Perry, then nervously at Olivia. Continuing he said, "the summary of the first message is that the House of Lords has closed its session with the various members leaving for home. Arguments over the missive from Arista resulted in a brawl on the floor of the House of Lords. A faction comprised of pre-unification Lords accused prince Justin of a power grab by stopping the wedding. Those backing prince Justin have the view that Lord Druango concocted this. His objective being to eliminate the prince so that when the marriage is consummated he can exercise control over the queen without interference. The rumors all have to do with pre-unification Lords forming militias under the guise of self-protection."

Perry caught, held the young man's eye and asked, "what do you think Lieutenant?"

Graves was ready for this question. General Eastbrook was famous for asking people at all levels in his army their opinion. Everyone knew there were no negative consequences when honestly answering. "None of it makes sense sir. Druango would have been better served to marry the queen and then act to take control." He glanced quickly and nervously at Olivia after delivering that opinion but then continued, "General Fedral assigned me as Prince Justin's military aide and my observation is that he's completely devoted to the queen. Even if he wasn't loyal, stopping the wedding in this fashion would be stupid, and the prince is anything but that."

When Lieutenant Graves finished giving his opinion Perry decided he was impressed. Justin had made a good decision sending this young man. He was an excellent communicator and insightful. Given he couldn't leave the ranch, Perry would add him to his personal staff. Perry then opened it up for discussion and questions. As the poor young lieutenant was being peppered by questions from all sides he excused himself and asked Olivia to accompany him. Walking to the buffet where the message packet had been placed he pulled the coded messages out and they retired to his office. After decoding the first message, they read.

*Olivia,*

*It's likely going to end in war. Not clear to me who kidnapped Bria or what their end game is. Druango is using this to stir up the former non-aligned regions. Given that Arista claims they will return 'the queen' he feels he has the upper hand in appealing to those who love her. The fact I openly rebelled against the king makes me look like the guilty one to many.*

*It's time to make some decisions. The first is whether to announce that the kidnappers missed. That Bria is the one being held by Arista.*

*The upside is that this would remove the excuse Druango has for building up the militias. The downside is that we don't know who is behind all of this and it's possible the revelation could play into their hands. Bria's safety is a large concern of mine in this scenario.*

*The second decision is whether to demand the newly formed militias be immediately disbanded. This is likely to launch a civil war. You both know my opinion on Lord Druango and the inevitability of conflict, so I won't bother to restate it.*

*My advice? Keep the fact that the kidnappers missed their target a secret. Authorize me as Regent to recall Perry as General of the Royal Armed Forces. I would further advise you to direct him to get on a war footing as soon as possible. If you agree with my advice I recommend you stay with the army and lay low until we can recover you safely.*

*Your faithful servant,*

*Justin*

Opening and decoding the second message they both read.

*Perry,*

*I know you're going to recommend we announce the queen's presence in Liberty and avoid an immediate war. Sacrifice for the greater good is in your nature. However, I caution you that war is sometimes the greater good. I believe that to be true in this instance. We will get Bria back, but we need your sacrifice along with hers until we are certain we understand who is pulling strings and what the end game is.*

*These messages were sent with Lieutenant Graves. He is an intelligent and unusually insightful young man. Take some time and question him before you send him back. I've found him to provide excellent observations and advice.*

*Your faithful friend,*

*Justin*

Perry sat with Olivia and they both thought about the new developments and what they meant. Olivia finally broke the silence by saying, "I agree with Justin's advice. My gut tells me I made a mistake trusting that Lord Druango could be controlled. My guess is that he's behind all this but agree with Lieutenant Graves that none of it makes sense."

Perry considered that for a moment and then responded, "the Commonwealth is involved in this somehow. There has to be a third player. They were acting behind the scenes with your father. That means Lord Druango is in league with them. Since the Commonwealth only cares about tax revenues this means whatever plan they have is not good for our people. My advice is…"

A loud crash sounding like a door being broken in was followed by breaking glass from the windows in the next room. The next thing they heard was a series of whistles. Peters always kept a whistle around his neck and used it on the battlefield to communicate commands to his rangers. This one was an order to converge on him if Perry remembered the commands correctly. Perry immediately motioned Olivia to stay put while going to his weapons rack and pulling out a short sword and long knife. Stopping for a moment he grabbed his cavalry saber as well. Rushing through his office door he was met with complete chaos. A melee was taking place in the dining room with Graves and Peters in the middle of it. Graves was the only one with a sword having brought it in when he arrived. Peters was a brawler. He was brandishing a chair as a defensive weapon to buy time. Perry yelled "Sword" at Peters while throwing the short sword handle first. Peters turned and grabbed the sword out of the air and went on the offensive, brandishing both sword and chair. Perry then caught Colonel Pike's eye and tossed him the cavalry sword. He stayed put in the doorway until Peters, Graves, Pike, and the rest of his staff were in danger of being overwhelmed. He yelled "Barricade the door," over his shoulder as he dove in.

Peters, Graves, and Pike were shoulder to shoulder bearing the brunt of the attack while the rest of his staff officers armed with table knives did what they could. Pike went down first followed soon after by Graves. This left Peters trying to hold all of the attackers off. Perry jumped in and grabbed Grave's sword and they reestablished a stalemate. Suddenly Perry was separated off and in danger of being overwhelmed. Peters, swaying on his feet from multiple stab wounds yelled in frustration and launched himself into the middle of the swarm of those around Perry. The rest of Perry's staff followed. All of a sudden the cutlery knives started spouting randomly in the attackers. This caused a lull in the fighting as the attackers struggled to adjust to this new threat. As Olivia started running out of table knives Peters rangers showed up in force. It was quickly over once they arrived.

Olivia hurried over to check on Pike who appeared to be badly injured. She had known him since she was a little girl. She checked his wounds, turned to Perry, and shook her head. There was a new opening on Perry's staff. Graves had a serious gash on his sword arm, but it was not life threatening. A blow to the head had knocked him out. He was now awake but a bit confused as he slowly recovered. She went to a battered and bloodied Peters. To her surprise she discovered he was still alive. He had clearly offered his life to the attackers in exchange for Perry's. Serious wounds but still living. "Get a doctor in here immediately," she ordered one of Perry's staff officers who only had a few minor injuries. Then she started compressing the more serious wounds using dinner napkins and strips of cloth from her dress.

"You shouldn't be doing this Bria," Peters said seriously.

Although she was extremely worried about him, she smiled at his discomfort of being cared for by his queen. It was amazing to her that he was clear-headed enough to maintain the ruse. She then said in a joking voice, "I'm a farm girl Timothy. I know how to take care of the animals."

Peters smiled with difficulty and then with an amused expression on his face said. "Thank you. You are truly an animal angel."

She realized they were flirting with each other. He seemed to have realized it as well to his embarrassment. It was even a bigger surprise when she realized how much she liked it. He was a very attractive man who she greatly enjoyed being around. His quick thinking and unwavering support immediately after the king had been killed had shown his intelligence and compassion. She also felt incredibly safe when he was around. Of course, any thoughts in that direction were worse than useless. She would marry for the kingdom, not for love. That was Bria's future, not hers.

The doctor showed up and gently guided her out of the way so he could get to work. She looked around the room and caught Perry's eye. He had been barking out orders getting some semblance of a defense organized and established around the house. She realized it might not be over yet. Still in a daze she looked further around the room and realized there were only eight attackers dead on the floor. It had seemed like so many more to her. Seeing Colonel Pike lying dead in a pool of blood was incredibly sad. Sadness slowly turned to anger. This was a man who had survived much hardship for the security of the kingdom. This was a man who had always been kind to her. He ought to have enjoyed his final years in peace. A peace he had fought hard and sacrificed much for. She resolved he would not die in vain. The kingdom would have peace.

Later when order had been established, and a careful sweep had been done around the ranch house, Olivia and Perry continued their conversation. Olivia looked at Perry with steel in her eyes and said, "I know you believe we ought to be compassionate with our enemies. That punishing them just leads to making sure they will always oppose us."

"Hold on Olivia," Perry said calmly, but with purpose in his voice. "It's true. I believe it's better to turn your enemy into your friend rather than punish them." Olivia started to break in, but Perry put his hand up stopping her. "But there are times when your enemy has proven they are evil. Sometimes all your attempts to redeem them fail." He paused as his face took on rock hard determination and he said, "it's time to salt the earth."

Olivia understood the biblical reference and shuttered

inside.

CHAPTER 19

# HARVEST FESTIVAL

The past four months of training with Victor had been hell. Battered and bruised, Tee was having a hard time seeing the benefit of getting beaten senseless every day. Every time he ended up in the dirt, or was declared dead, Victor would tell him in colorful language what he had done wrong. Then they would focus on specific exercises intended to fix that specific deficiency. Every one of his weaknesses was attacked over and over and over again until Victor was satisfied.

After one such session Tee had been visibly frustrated and angry. Instead of consoling him Victor said, "size and strength are useful, but it's not what separates good fighters from mediocre ones. It's what you have between your ears that matters. You don't suffer from a lack of size; you suffer from letting your stature be your excuse. You're surprisingly tough Tee, but you have to stop giving yourself excuses."

At first Victors lecture just made him angrier. Heartless asshole thought Tee. But calming down later he reluctantly admitted to himself that it was true. His whole life others had told him his lack of size and strength meant he had limitations. He was guilty of accepting this. It wasn't their fault for having an opinion. It was his fault in accepting that opinion and making it his own.

Oddly enough the next morning Victors accusation was starkly confirmed. Someone unfamiliar was sparring with Victor. Although smaller than Tee, he was challenging Victor and making him work. Not that the stranger was anywhere close to winning, but he did make it interesting.

When the time came for Tee's daily training regimen he asked, "Who's the guy you were sparring with this morning? I thought you didn't spar with the other gladiators."

"His name is Forti. He's not a gladiator, He's a citizen. Won thirty bouts in the Arena and was given his freedom," Victor said.

"If he's a citizen why is he here?" Tee asked.

"He wants to keep his fighting skills sharp. He's the head of Senator Cereo's security team and assassination attempts are common here," Victor answered. He then added, "and he's a friend."

"You have a friend?" Tee asked, before realizing how that sounded.

Victor laughed loudly causing the other gladiators to glance over at them. Then continuing to smile he said, "yes, I am human Tee." Then settling back into his normal training voice, he said, "and being human I am sometimes a hypocrite. I didn't learn my lesson right away. When I first got here the other gladiators would challenge me. It was irritating since I had nothing to gain from sparring with them. I would accept their challenge and make the experience as painful as possible without losing my exercise yard rights. That caused them to leave me alone. It didn't work with Forti. He kept coming back. So, I asked him, "do you have a pain fetish?""

Instead of being insulted he laughed and said, "no, perhaps a lack of brains, but no fetishes." Then he looked me in the eye and said, "winning doesn't make me better. Only losing does that." This was a man I could respect. I became his mentor and eventually his friend. He claims he gained his freedom because of me. It would have been horrible if I had been forced to meet him in the Arena. Thank God that didn't happen."

Tee's natural stubbornness took over at that point. He was guilty of exactly what Victor had accused him of. He pledged that his excuses for himself were going to stop. Once he accepted this he started to progress rapidly, surprising even Victor. Instead of backing off Victor pushed harder, became more intense. When he first realized Victor had not been going full speed it momentarily depressed him. Then he realized the change in Victor was a compliment, so he worked even harder.

Then one day it happened, Tee knocked Victor to the ground. As he moved in for the kill Victor rolled quickly to the side and up and then put him down, match over. Instead of frowning, Victor smiled. Helping Tee up he said, "I've been waiting for the right time to tell you this. You have progressed from being an embarrassment to being adequate." Then holding up one hand he said, "Before you start puffing up your feathers you still aren't what I would call good. Not even close."

Tee was bursting with pride at that announcement. He knew he was much better than he had been when he left Pacifica. It made the last few months of pain and embarrassment worth it.

"Now we're going to focus on something you're already much better at than most. Paying attention," Victor said. "I lied when I said size and strength don't matter, they do. But I'm not a good fighter because of physical attributes. It's because I pay attention."

Victor then started spending time coaching Tee on what to look for in weaknesses. Tee always thought this was a strength of his, and it was, but he quickly discovered it wasn't nearly as refined as it could be. Victor was an expert in human anatomy. He could watch you walk and know the condition of your ankles, knees, hips, and back. All of which might have potential weaknesses to exploit. He passed on this knowledge constantly testing Tee whenever someone new showed up. It didn't have to be a gladiator, anyone could be analyzed, taken apart, and exposed.

After the initial lecturing on this Victor started imitating a variety of weaknesses. Bad knee, sore back, stiff hip, etc. Tee was expected to immediately identify the vulnerability and quickly devise a plan to take advantage of it. Once he had devised an acceptable plan he had to practice it over and over and over again. No detail was too obscure. No advantage too small.

One day Victor pulled Tee off to the side and asked, "What are Sam's weaknesses?" Sam had only been there a few days but had immediately gone to the Arena and survived.

"He isn't bilateral. Attacks primarily with his right side, sword, strike, and kick. His right shoulder appears to be damaged as he doesn't lift it all the way over his head. He ducks with his arm at an odd angle when faced with a high attack on that side," Tee explained.

"How would you attack him?" Victor said.

"Force him into a block with his right arm high. He will likely adjust rotating to his right and lowering his center of balance. Depending on how his stance changes would determine the next move," Tee said.

"Wrong," Victor said. "Part of the reason you believe this is you've seen him get caught off balance during sparring." Hesitating Victor then asked, "what weapons did Sam have on him when he went to the Arena?"

"Sword, round shield, long knife," Tee said looking a bit confused.

"How did he sheath his long knife?" Victor asked.

"Where it's easy to grab with his left hand," Tee answered. Frowning in concentration his face took on a knowing look. "He's fooling the other gladiators into thinking he has a weakness he doesn't have."

Victor nodded his head pleased. "There isn't anything wrong with his shoulder. The other secret he hides is that he's ambidextrous. I saw Eric toss him a knife and he grabbed it out of the air effortlessly with his left hand without thinking about it. I saw him frown slightly as he realized he had screwed up. Don't just watch them fighting, watch everything."

"So now how would you attack Sam," Victor asked.

"Same way, except the high strike would be a feint to try and get him to commit to dropping his shield and attacking with his knife hand. Since he would think he has me fooled he might be coaxed into overextending. But I wouldn't rely on surprise or assume I have him fooled. Now that he's shown himself to be clever I need to consider that any scenario might have been part of his overall plan," Tee said.

Victor nodded, obviously pleased with that answer. "The smart ones are the dangerous ones Tee. Make sure you study that aspect of your enemies even most closely than their physical traits."

Victor then took a deep breath, let it out, and then said, "tonight is the last night of the Harvest Festival. It's traditional to get a special meal tonight. Way more than anyone needs. Wine will be offered as well. "Don't make the mistake of overeating or having anything other than water to drink tonight. You'll go to the Arena tomorrow and the last thing you need is to be weighed down and sluggish because you overindulged," Victor said.

Of course, Victor had advice about dinner, Tee thought, he had advice about everything. "Yes master," Tee said sarcastically. Their relationship had improved since he had been deemed barely adequate. Tee could even joke around with him a bit. He was nervous about going into the Arena the next day and nervousness tended to heighten his sarcasm. He was a bit touched by the fact that Victor seemed to care what happened to him in the Arena and that tended to heighten his sarcastic nature as well.

"Don't be a smart ass," Victor said bluntly and walked away.

The next day while he was getting suited up Victor was all business, "get stretched out but save your energy for the Arena." Victor hesitated locking eyes with him and said "Remember what I told you. Take them out as quickly as you can without overreaching. It's a blessing for them if it's quick. Anyone injured who stops fighting disappoints the emperor and they die a very painful death later." Taking a deep breath, he said in a low voice only Tee could hear. "Forti told me they are going to release three at a time and a total of five groups. Not clear if it's on a schedule or whenever you dispatch the previous three. There are hidden doors in the walls so they can appear at any time from any direction. Listen to the crowd. If you hear anything new, a change in volume or tone, quickly check your surroundings."

Tee just nodded his head. Now wasn't the time for jokes. The only thing new was that he would be facing five groups of gladiators three at a time. The fact that Victor was repeating himself told Tee how concerned he was.

As he was being led to the tunnel system leading underground to the Arena he stopped and simply said, "thank you Victor."

Victor hesitated, grabbed Tees shoulders with both of his hands, turned him around, and then locking eyes with him said in a whisper, "Ad Victoriam."

Tee stood a little stunned and went weak in the knees. He hadn't expected this. Taking a deep breath and squaring his shoulders, he gave the correct response. "Cum scuto aut in scuto". Victor gave him a quick nod, patted his shoulders, turned around, and walked away.

It wasn't Tee's first battle as a member of the Guard. It was his first appearance in the Arena. Performing the ritual was not strictly appropriate. But Victor was sending multiple messages by claiming the honor of a mentor. It meant Victor truly respected him. That Tee was necessary for winning the battle and Victor would be honored to fight alongside him. It was a message that they were still of the Guard and Arista was the enemy. 'To Victory' meant much more than an inspirational message. It was a reminder they were committed to ultimate victory. Or at the very least, in Victors own words, making sure the bastards pay. It had the intended effect; Tee was committed to victory beyond simply preserving his life.

Tee couldn't see the Arena from the holding cell they had him in awaiting his bout. But he could hear. The festivities started off with a man loudly begging for mercy, then screaming in pain, followed by more begging. This progressed to deep mournful sobs and ultimately a plea for death. It seemed an eternity before that plea was answered. Tee was disgusted by the audible enjoyment of the crowd. The next hour was spent listening to a series of bouts being played out with the occasional roar from the crowd. He supposed it was an advantage to hear all this. It prepared him for what would follow.

When his time came Tee walked purposely down the corridor to the Arena. He could feel the excitement in the waiting crowd. As he walked out onto the Arena floor a roar went up that he not only heard but felt. His eyes struggled to adjust to the brightness and when he was able to see clearly the sight stunned him. He had never seen so many people in one place. This was his first time seeing the inside of the Arena. The seating had multiple levels that rose steeply into a cloudless blue sky. Looking at the packed sand floor of the Arena he saw blood stains scattered here and there. There were discarded weapons strewn around as well. Perhaps the weapons of the defeated. He would have to pay attention as he could trip over them, or his opponents could pick them up and use them. He knew this was the final bout of the harvest festival. They called it the finale. He located the emperor's box. It was one level up but directly across from him. The emperor was easy to spot. He sat in the middle, richly adorned, and had a smug smile that suggested the truth of what Tee had heard. This man had no morals.

Tee walked forward and positioned himself in front of the emperor. Having been coached on what to do he took his right fist and slammed it against his chest in a salute and loudly declared "for the honor of Emperor Trajan." At the same time thinking to himself that this man had no honor.

The Emperor was seemingly bored with Tee's

declaration. He maintained his smug smile as he made a shooing motion indicating the bout should begin.

Tee moved to the middle of the Arena and slowly turned around waiting for things to start. He cautioned himself to ignore the crowd. Except as an audible indication of what he wasn't currently seeing. A shout went up and he whipped around as a gate behind him opened up and three men came out. All had small round shields but two had swords and one had a spear. He didn't recognize any of them. Victor had told him that he would likely see a combination of criminals, captured warriors, and gladiators he was very familiar with. Warriors who were captured but not purchased as professional gladiators were unlikely to be highly skilled. Criminals were often sent out who hadn't even held a weapon before. For the most part he needed to worry most about those he saw every day. However, there were exceptions, so he was cautioned to be careful.

The three rushed forward spreading out in an obvious attempt to surround him. Their haste indicated they were more afraid of the emperor's wrath than Tee. All three looked terrified. Tee let them separate then he rushed the one who held his weapon as if he knew how to use it. He purposely forced the man to turn so he could engage while still keeping an eye on the other two. The man was dead in seconds. The other two yelled and tried to rush him together. It was over quickly, none of them having much skill.

Tee moved towards the emperor's box suggesting he was ready to accept his victory. The emperor shooed him back indicating his day wasn't over yet. Victor said it was important to protect Forti, so he played out the ruse. They could not allow any indication that he had been coached on what to expect.

Tee quickly moved back into the center of the Arena and started his slow turn waiting for whatever was coming next. He glanced up at the emperor and got a nod of approval which just made him feel sick. It was an abomination to be a part of this disgusting entertainment. This time two came out from the same gate he had entered by. He heard the crowd grow quieter. Alarmed Tee whipped around and caught the third of this set trying to sneak up behind him. He charged the lone gladiator eliminating one threat before the other two could converge. Again, it was over quickly. None of his opponents had been capable of causing concern.

It wasn't until the fourth set that a real challenge emerged. Two of the three were men he was familiar with. They weren't the best of the gladiators, but they were skilled and thus dangerous. They also stayed together instead of spreading apart. He dispatched the loner and then had a protracted fight against the two gladiators. They had a good, coordinated plan to wear him down. He was forced to fight them both at the same time, which drew out the fight. He eventually prevailed with one minor cut on his upper arm. When he was pinked the crowd erupted. They had evidently become bored with the slaughter and wanted some of his blood as well.

He was breathing deeply and feeling his legs when the last three came out of the gate just below the emperor's box. They were the three best gladiators in the yard. Having knowledge of them was a double-edged sword. While he knew them, they knew him. They had been watching his bouts with Victor for months. The other advantage they had was his inexperience in fighting smaller men. Victor had insisted he spend as much time as possible sparring with Forti, the only other sparring he allowed. However, Forti's availability was sporadic, and it wasn't the same as regular bouts with various fighters of that size.

These three stayed together mirroring the strategy of the prior group. Two of them were armed with spears and the third was armed with a sword. The spears were on the outside and the swordsman on the inside. They marched forward together. Searching for anything to give him an advantage he noticed a large rectangular shield that had been left from a previous bout. He picked it up and charged. This caused the spearmen to extend their spears, which he was relying on. As he engaged he swept the spears off to the side with his sword causing them all to react by retreating a few steps in unison to reestablish their defense. Instead of stopping he swiveled the shield sideways in mid stride and barreled into the tightly packed group of three before they got set.

There was a lot that could have gone wrong with this tactic. But it seemed luck was on his side. Instead of getting tangled up in the pile of bodies he rolled clear. Popping up he immediately dispatched one of the two spearmen before the unfortunate man could regain his bearings. The crowd roared its approval, evidently enjoying his trick. The next few minutes were exhausting, and he decided to take more of a defensive posture. It was a gamble, if another three emerged before he dispatched these two his life was likely over. He prayed Forti was a trustworthy source as he waited for his opponents to make a mistake. The spearman stumbled slightly on a piece of equipment left behind from one of the earlier groups and lost his right hand as a consequence. This left him face to face with Sam. Everything Victor had suspected about Sam had been confirmed during the fight so far. Strikes and lunges intended to subtly test his supposed weaknesses convinced Tee those weaknesses were a ruse. Trusting his instincts, he attacked as if Sam had a bad shoulder and was rewarded with a knife attack from Sam's left hand. Sam's head flew off his body to the raucous approval of the crowd.

Instead of immediately going forward for the emperor's approval he turned and walked purposely back to the spearman who had lost a hand. The man was still alive and in shock. Tee was not going to leave the poor man to suffer whatever sick torture was in store for him. What he had heard earlier had hardened his resolve that he would only go so far with this travesty. He drove his sword into the man's chest ending his suffering. The crowd roared its approval.

He went back to the center of the arena and holding his sword and shield up screamed out a challenge for the next test. When he had turned around enough to see the emperor the man motioned him to come towards him. Tee positioned himself in front of the emperor's box and saluted with his fist to his chest waiting for a decision. The emperor frowned and hesitated. Any wounded who stopped fighting were supposed to be left for the emperor's judgement. Or perhaps more accurately, the emperor's enjoyment. Perhaps thinking Tee didn't know the correct protocol yet, he smiled and said in a loud voice. "One."

Twenty-nine more wins and I gain my freedom, thought Tee with disgust. He knew his freedom would never be allowed but he would play along with their tradition.

"Twenty-nine," he shouted bringing the crowd back to its feet and cheering him on as he walked off.

Victor greeted him as he entered the gladiator's compound. "Am happy to see you survived. Pray for those you were forced to kill today. They are not our enemies." When Tee nodded his understanding Victor added, "Forti watched your matches today. He'll stop by tomorrow so we can review your performance. Rest." And with that Victor walked off with a sad look on his face.

Tee was deeply troubled. He sat reflecting on the men he had faced. He had no idea how many GEMs he had killed. But today's fifteen deaths laid heavily on his conscience. Protecting himself and others didn't hold any regrets for him. But what had happened today bothered him to his core. He knew their faces would show up in his nightmares and guilt over their deaths would not go away. Victor had told him a quick killing was a blessing for those men since the alternative was a long and protracted death full of pain and suffering. But it just felt wrong. And it always would.

A beautiful young woman was brought to his cell that evening. She had a light sheer cloak on and nothing else. There were catcalls from the other gladiators as she had made her way down the hall. Tee noticed that Dobler was clearly unhappy with his role in bringing her but was trying not to let it show. Tee had become even better at reading people due to Victor's training. His already good opinion of Dobler was further enhanced.

Dobler stopped in front of his cell and spit out, "the emperor was appreciative of your efforts today. This is your reward." Then he unlocked Tee's cell door and gently encouraged the girl to enter. Saying nothing further, he locked the door behind her and walked back down the hallway.

The poor girl was trembling. He towered over her. Tee knew how intimidating that must be. His blood was boiling. He tried to keep the rage off his face. She was frightened enough already. Tee was grateful that Victor had warned him of this. Her knuckles were white, and her hands shook as she gripped the cloak high on her chest. When she tentatively started to open her cloak he stepped forward, closed it firmly, and said softly, "I'm not going to abuse you." Then he turned grabbed one of his robes and draped it over her motioning her to pull it closed as well.

"It's too cold in here for just that. My name is Tee, what's yours?" Tee said.

"Ca, Ca, Cara sir," she finally got out. Then with tears pooling in her eyes she said, "they will beat me or worse if I don't satisfy you." The poor girl was terrified.

He considered what to say and then responded with, "Cara, I'll tell them you satisfied me. I'll ask if you can stay longer and if you can come back from time to time." He hesitated and then lifted her head with a gentle lift with his fingers on her chin. Locking eyes with her he said, "where I come from we don't believe in slavery. We do not abuse women. You're safe here."

That seemed to give her hope, but she was still trembling. He hesitated and then said, "my grandmother always says to find something to enjoy even in the worst of times. She believes being happy is a choice not a result of circumstances. I've found her advice to be very wise." The girl looked at him like he was crazy. That was clearly not the right thing to say. Great Tee, he thought. Way to make her relax. He sighed and thought that perhaps she would consider Grammy's advice at another time. Grammy or Hestie would have known what to say. God he missed them both at times like these. Feeling incompetent he considered how to make the poor girl more comfortable. He ended up giving her the bed and sleeping on the floor. Turned out ignoring her was the best thing he could do.

Dobler knew something was going on. Victor and Tee were up to something. He didn't know what, but he knew he should report the various inconsistencies and oddities he was seeing. His life depended on it. But some things were more important to him than his empty life. His wife and youngest daughter had been captured along with himself by slavers years ago. The girl the emperor had supplied as a reward for Tee's Arena performance looked just like his daughter had at that age. Could have been her twin. It broke his heart when she showed up.

Dobler was not surprised to discover the next morning that Tee had treated the girl with respect. He realized he would have been surprised if he hadn't. Victor had always done the same with the girls supplied. Not that Tee admitted it. No, Tee had told him enthusiastically that the girl had 'greatly satisfied' him. He turned a little red at that point and then requested she stay with him for longer. It was a bit too enthusiastic, and the slight blush didn't help. The look on the girl's face ratted him out as well. It was heartwarming. Tee had gone to much trouble to try and provide the poor girl with a few hours of decency. Tee was scary as hell. Almost as scary as Victor. He was a horrible liar. But clearly an honorable man. Dobler thought he had gotten the measure of Tee from their late-night talks. This confirmed his suspicions. He didn't know where his wife or daughter were. The last he saw of either of them was at the slave auction. His image of them being led off the auction block by different owners was burned into his brain. He prayed nightly that they had found some semblance of happiness.

Later that day Leo, Senator Cereo's valet, showed up to collect the girl and ask about Tee. "Did you see Tee fight in the Arena?" Leo asked with enthusiasm.

Dobler looked down at the tabletop in front of him and said, "no, I never watch the Arena fights. I'm around the gladiators so much I get too attached." The truth was that he was disgusted by the Arena and everything it represented.

"Too bad, it was a once in a lifetime experience. Everyone will be talking about it for months. The emperor decided to test our new Pacifica gladiator. He told people beforehand he wanted to find out how tough he really was. Tee did not disappoint. Fifteen dead in a little over 15 minutes. They were released three at a time and told they would be part of the after games entertainment if they didn't engage quickly," Leo said.

So, a choice between a quick death and an excruciatingly painful one thought Dobler. He nodded his understanding and waited to see if Leo had anything else to say.

"How did Tee like the emperors gift?" Leo asked with a knowing smile.

The emperor was known for awarding the owners of the winning gladiators for special events with beautiful and untouched newly captured slaves. The understanding was that the gladiator got to go first. It was too much for Dobler. She reminded him too much of his daughter and he was outraged. He had lived long enough. Years of frustration caused him to drop his façade and say, "your gladiator is a better person than that. He was respectful of the girl. He refused to take advantage of her. He might be a slave, but he has morals. More than you can say about most citizens of Arista." He was dead. Perhaps it was for the best he thought. His life had been better than most. But it was getting increasingly harder to accept the tradeoffs.

Leo's expression surprisingly changed from haughty to concerned. He hesitated, clearly thinking about his response. Then he said, "I'm not going to report your outburst. But I will tell you something in return that I trust you'll keep between us." Leo stopped waiting for an acknowledgment from Dobler. When Dobler nodded his head he continued, "Senator Cereo will not be informed of Tee's behavior or your comments. Given your concerns about the girl I'll tell you that he doesn't allow his slaves to interact with anyone at his Roma Domus. Do their job yes, interact with others no. We'll move her into his Domus as a serving girl and maid. She will be safe, at least until she's moved to his villa."

Dobler was stunned and he took a few moments to collect himself and consider what had been said. He took a deep breath and dived in saying, "Tee requested she stay with him longer and be sent to him on a regular basis. He's trying to provide a place for her to occasionally relax and feel safe. He thinks he's fooling me, but he's not."

"That won't be possible. As I said, Senator Cereo doesn't allow his slaves to interact with others, even other slaves. Security is a serious issue for him. For the same reason he never sells his slaves. I trust you will keep this between us Dobler," Leo said staring him down.

Well, that sounded better than the typical fate of a pretty young slave girl thought Dobler. He nodded his understanding and agreement then walked Leo out to the exit gate.

"Anything said between us stays between us," Dobler said.

"Thank you. I don't see a need to come around often. It seems like Tee is getting what he needs. But, let me know if there is anything you think he needs."

Dobler considered the conversation with Leo and wondered about it. His sudden change in demeaner was a surprise. Perhaps the man had his own secrets. He thought he would check in on Tee and wandered up to the recreation yard observation room. Eric was watching Tee practice his archery. There were arrows in the barrier wall behind the target and a few on the outer edges of the target. One had surprisingly hit dead center. "He is hopeless with a bow," Eric said smirking. "The others won't even run on the track when he's out there," he continued chuckling. "The one in the bullseye was Victor challenging him to hit the same section on the barrier wall an earlier arrow had hit. He's a demon with every other weapon, but a duel with bows and arrows at a hundred feet would favor me."

Dobler nodded his head. Then he narrowed his eyes in thought.

As he was walking Tee back to his cell Dobler casually said, "your archery isn't improving. Try relaxing your arms as much as you can and release the arrows smoothly. Use the same motion and rhythm every time. I'm not sure you'll ever be any good, archers are born, but you should be able to improve."

Tee froze inside, hiding his reaction as he thought about this. Dobler had been a frequent visitor to his cell at night. Tee knew Dobler had been a warrior as a young man. He also knew Dobler had little to no experience with archery. Dobler had never given him advice before either. It was obvious he knew Tee was faking his incompetence. No matter how bad someone was, practice would improve their skills. Tee mentally flogged himself and then calmly said. "Thanks, Dobler, I'll try that the next time I practice." Dobler nodded his head as he locked Tee into his cell. He hid a smile as he turned away and started walking back down the corridor.

CHAPTER 20

# NEWS FEED

Jennifer looked around the table and gave all the Committee members 'the look'. This was combined with a warm smile that made you want to pay attention. She had this way of getting people to stop their private conversations without being blunt about it, without saying a word. One of her many subtle skills. Once she had everyone's attention she said, "I want to start by thanking everyone for getting up extra early this morning. The Council is still in an uproar over issues surrounding the delayed planting and I have a full day with them starting right after this meeting." Jennifer paused and her face brightened a bit. "The good news is that the current crisis is pulling everyone together. A significant number of Landfall and Apple folks volunteered their labor to help make up for Eureka's late start to planting. I also want to thank Griff and Del one more time for assigning Guard and university students to help out as well."

"It's good for them," Griff said with a mischievous grin. "They need a reminder of where their food comes from."

"And it dispels the idea that farmers have it easy," Del added with his own grin.

Jennifer smiled inside. She knew they both grew up on farms and were a bit disdainful of those who hadn't. Although she grew up in the city, she agreed that city folk generally have it easier. Jennifer was no stranger to hard work. But spending summer 'vacations' on her relatives' farms meant she knew what life was really like on the farm.

Jennifer continued, "Not only will those efforts pay off in improving our food supply but the tension between the regions has gone down dramatically. I've been told by several people that the mistrust of the university and Guard that began with the call for full mobilization has gone away as well. I'm hopeful it will last. The bad news is we are going to have to ration. It's not nearly as bad as we originally thought, thanks to everyone pulling together. But we will have to be frugal with our food supply until the fall harvest next year. The other issue you all know about is heating oil. Everyone will have to wear extra layers this winter." Jennifer looked at Griff when she said this. She had false accusation in her tone and amusement in her eyes and everyone chuckled. Del had been right. Now that she knew Griff better she had grown to trust, like, and admire him.

Jennifer turned back to the group and said, "We only have one item on the agenda today. Del will review the latest intercepted communications and offer opinions on what it might mean. This is informational only. As I understand it there aren't any actions being proposed."

Del had a worried look on his face as he started his report. "Jennifer's correct. While there isn't anything of immediate concern there was a report transmitted on the GEM's that is alarming. The anthropologist who studies Pacifica cultures is claiming that the GEM's are evolving their social interactions. The latest report claims they are becoming more collaborative. Even more disturbing is the claim they are markedly more compliant to orders given by their leaders. The report stated that their common warriors 'don't need to be beaten into submission anymore'."

Griff grunted and said, "when you read accounts of battles with the GEMs over the past two hundred years you see a steady change that aligns with that view. Even a hundred years ago it wasn't unusual for an attack on the Wall to stop because the GEM's started killing each other instead of trying to kill us. Most recently it was clear that the attempted Apple Valley invasion was a joint exercise between two war lords. Their struggles to coordinate have always been one of our main advantages."

Del nodded his head in agreement and continued, "the report did confirm that we hurt the GEMs badly. While their main army isn't dispersing as usual, they are currently in no shape to organize another attack. It was clear that the author of this report was angry with our success. It's odd and I don't have an explanation for it."

"Maybe he just wants to go home," offered Kevin.

"Perhaps. But it is concerning that at least this one individual sees some sort of advantage to our demise. I'll continue to look for clues to help us sort out their motivations. But given the sporadic nature of our intercepts I don't have a lot of confidence in getting a firm answer."

"Why are the intercepts sporadic?" asked Griff.

"Good question." Del said with a smirk which Griff returned. Jennifer found it mildly annoying when the two of them bantered back and forth without explaining what their private joke was. Del then replaced the smirk with his professor's personality and explained, "The communications network consists of a system of satellites orbiting Pacifica. You can actually see them as tiny dots zipping across the sky on a moonless night. They communicate with each other and any spaceship in the vicinity with lasers. We don't have the ability to intercept those signals. However, these satellites also have microwave radios that transmit everything going over the network to the ground. We think it's there to support occasional visits to the surface for survey purposes. That signal we can collect. The reason our information is sporadic is twofold. First, all official Commonwealth traffic is encrypted with something we're not familiar with. We've tried to crack it over the years but have been unsuccessful. However, the Commonwealth requires personal communications to be transmitted with an encryption scheme we can decrypt. It's a simple one and easy to crack. I believe the Commonwealth doesn't trust its citizens. I believe they listen in on all personal communications. The second reason is that survey ships aren't always in orbit around Pacifica. They only come when they believe something interesting is happening or is about to happen. When they aren't here there are no communications to listen in on."

"So that means we're only getting their private letters to each other?" Jennifer asked.

Del's head nodded as he answered, "basically, yes. That and what they call news feeds. Their version of a newspaper." Del hesitated a second and added, "speaking of news feeds. There was some good news about Tee Stone. Well relatively good. He was reported to have survived his first visit to the Arena as a gladiator. I have a copy of the news article that goes into some detail. Evidently he fought a total of fifteen individuals and defeated them all. The article seemed to indicate that Commonwealth citizens can somehow watch these events."

Griff huffed out his disapproval and said, "thanks for showing me that earlier Del. It makes me angry to know those bastards find human suffering and death entertaining. But it's good to know Tee's still alive. Even better to know the competition is obviously not very good. Tee was never the best at hand-to-hand combat,"

"Why would an anthropologists report be sent in a personal communication?" Jennifer asked. "Are all of their survey reports sent that way?"

"No, we don't believe they are. It's also interesting that these reports are only being sent to one recipient. We don't know why," Del answered.

"How is Hestie working out?" Jennifer asked Del while looking sideways at Dorothy. That she could see an emotional reaction from the woman worried her a little.

Del shot a quick look over at Dorothy as well and then answered, "Perfectly. Quinn needed someone who could keep up with him on a few of his special projects. While I knew her biological knowledge was excellent, I was surprised by her knowledge of math and physics. It's obvious she's been hiding her abilities."

There was a pause in the conversation and then Dorothy stated bluntly, "Phillis Osman is asking questions."

"What kind of questions?" Jennifer asked.

"She named the five of us and asked me what we're doing in secret," Dorothy answered.

"Damn it!" Del said loudly before he could catch himself. "Sorry, that slipped out. I swear that woman is a mind reader. I do everything I can to avoid her but obviously she's picking up on something."

"It's not just you Del," Kevin piped in. "I've found myself telling her all kinds of things I didn't intend to say. Nothing about the committee or the Commonwealth but plenty about other concerns."

"What did you tell her?" asked Jennifer.

"The truth." Dorothy answered blandly. The room expelled a collective gasp. Then she calmly added, "I told her we are of like minds and discuss the challenges of Pacifica. I told her we meet to brainstorm."

"What did she say to that?"

"She asked if she could join. I told her it was invitation only and we already had university representation. I asked her to keep our groups existence a secret and she agreed." Dorothy responded, seemingly nonplussed by the whole thing.

Del let out a deep breath then said, "I've actually thought quite a bit about situations where she might be useful. I concluded she would be perfect as an advisor on a negotiation team. Perhaps negotiating with the Commonwealth if that ever came to pass. Her ability to manipulate people without them knowing they are being manipulated is unbelievable."

"Can we trust her to keep what she knows secret?" Jennifer asked.

Del and Dorothy both said simultaneously, "yes."

Jennifer gave that some thought and then said, "Ok. Del I would like you to engage her on this and set up regular meeting to hear her thoughts on the big challenges we face as a people. We either need to keep engaged with her or ask her to join. I'm reluctant to add anyone simply to keep them quiet. Let's add an agenda item to discuss how we ensure she is seen as the leader of Pacifica if the Commonwealth comes in and we're all, um, unavailable." Jennifer paused and then said, "I think that's it for today. We'll still meet at the regular time because I think I'll have news from the Council to discuss."

Del was distressed about having to meet regularly with Phillis. That woman is going to break down my barriers one of these days, he thought to himself. "Griff, stay here for a few minutes. I have something to discuss. I'll be right back." Griff just nodded his head and sat back down.

The door opened a few minutes later and Del had Quinn in tow. He sat down and said, "I've been keeping one last secret from you. Quinn knows and it's time you know too."

CHAPTER 21

# WINE TASTING

The Governor and First Minister were riding in an opulent carriage in the early evening on their way to Domus Cereo. They passed through the squalor of the inner city and entered an exclusive neighborhood with elaborate gas streetlamps. The lamps cast a pleasing warm light bright enough to hint at the elegance of large mansions on both sides of the road. Governor Jacobs was not used to primitive transportation having spent most of her career on Commonwealth planets. The colonies did not have the cars, trains, and shuttle craft commonly used by Commonwealth citizens.

"What's that horrible smell?" Governor Jacobs asked wrinkling her nose.

"It's a mixture of dung and horse sweat," Jack answered. He hesitated a moment and then added, "if you're around it long enough you get used to it."

"Gross." Said Jacobs wrinkling her nose. Looking over at him she asked, "tell me a little about tonight's event."

"It's a special wine tasting hosted by Dry Brook Vineyards. That's Senator Cereo's foundational business. It's what took him from poverty to a serious businessman," Jack explained. "There will be a mix of politicians, business magnates, plus ladies and gentlemen of leisure in attendance. It's invitation only so it won't be a large crowd. Senator Cereo is really good at using these events to endear himself to the elite and the poor. Every year they pull out a small number of older vintages of a wine called Jenny's Acre and auction them off for a homeless charity. This year's highlight is a single bottle from his first vintage. Bidding will be fierce."

"How did you get an invitation? The governor asked.

"I think it's his way of signaling that he wants alignment with the Commonwealth. His friends and enemies will notice the Commonwealth's presence. It's a political statement if nothing else. After his initial surprise he'll see your arrival as a boon to his prestige. Everyone will assume he has a working relationship with you and the rumors will fly. It should give us an advantage in negotiations. Perception is everything with these people," Jack said with a smile.

"We've established he's smart. Let's see if he has balls," Jacobs replied with a predatory smile.

The carriage pulled up to an elegant Domus with its own gas-powered lamps providing added illumination to its entrance. A large number of security personnel protected the narrow entry to the drive. They were allowed to proceed up the drive after showing their fancy printed invitation.

*Dry Brook Vineyards is pleased to invite*

*Jack Spenser and Guest*

*to its annual auction for the hungry*

*featuring the first vintage of Jenny's Acre*

After pulling up in front of the entry they were met by liveried footmen opening their carriage door. One of them offered to help Governor Jacobs out. Receiving an icy glare, and a sharp wave of her hand, he backed off letting her navigate her own way out of the conveyance. Governor Jacobs did not like anyone helping her, especially men.

Domus Cereo wasn't the largest or grandest in Roma. But it was impressive. Jack had been told it was the original Cereo hereditary home lost by Senator Cereo's parents in bankruptcy. Evidently the senator had reacquired the property once he had the financial resources to do so. Handing over the printed invitation they were allowed to enter the large double doors at the entrance. The massive entry hall was an odd combination of grandeur coupled with a feeling you were actually visiting someone's home. In Jacks experience most of these grand mansions had a cold clinical feel to them. This one was somehow warm and inviting. Remembering his last visit, he told the butler they could find the library on their own. The library was a good-sized hall set up for entertainment and could comfortably hold up to fifty people. It was much smaller than the ballroom he had been escorted to for the last party. It had a cozier more intimate feel to it.

Senator Cereo greeted them with a smile at the doorway to the library. "Welcome back to my home Jack, always good to see you," he said. Turning to Governor Jacobs he introduced himself. "My name is Caius Cereo Governor. I am delighted you were able to join us for our Dry Brook wine tasting. Please call me Caius."

"Delighted to meet you Caius. I do enjoy a good glass of wine so I'm looking forward to the evening," the governor said as she smiled and surveyed her prey. She had a way of making people uncomfortable even when saying all the right things.

"I hope you don't mind but I have a private room set up for discussions with Jack after the auction. Obviously, you are welcome to join us," Caius said seemingly nonplussed with the governor's body language. Most people visibly wilted when she openly broadcast her predatory nature. Jacks respect for Caius grew. Caius turned and swept his arm across the room saying. "Please visit the various tables. Each one is dedicated to a particular wine. Each table has an expert to answer your questions. They also have small plates that pair well with that particular wine. If you start just to your left and follow the tables around the room you'll get the best experience. But feel free to wander. Olympia is our winemaker. She's the woman over by the fireplace holding court. Enjoy."

They spent the next half hour wandering around the

room with Jack introducing people to the governor. As always, she was gracious but intense. She had a way of impressing and intimidating people all at the same time. Jack knew she liked wine but was surprised how much she was enjoying the experience. He decided he needed to learn more about wine as it was the first non-work topic she seemed to enjoy. Jack started to relax as she was almost purring with her enjoyment of the event.

They were introduced to Senator File who was Caius Cereo's longtime wine distributor. The governor immediately started an aggressive interrogation of the older gentleman with questions about Cereo's businesses. Jack was amused by the man's ability to divert her questions. As she was breaking down his walls Caius approached with a man in tow. Jack froze, paralyzed as Caius announced his guest, "Governor Jacobs, I found Chief Justice Evans wandering around."

Evans was Jacob's rival in the sector. They hated each other. This was the first time Jack had ever seen Jacobs caught off guard. However, she recovered quickly and said "Justice Evans, what a pleasure to see you. I had no idea you were here on Arista."

"I've been a fan of Dry Brook Vineyards since discovering it last year. Senator Cereo was kind enough to invite me and I decided to accept," Evans said with a lightly flushed face broadcasting an overindulgence in the evening's entertainment.

"I told Justice Evans we were going to discuss the current situation with Liberty tonight and he asked to attend. I hope I didn't overstep," Senator Caius said with an air of innocence and subservience that was completely believable.

"It's wonderful the good Justice is here tonight. By all means he should attend if he isn't otherwise engaged. We want to ensure that all Commonwealth Edicts are strictly followed. I wouldn't want anyone on Arista to have an accidental violation that would cause work for his organization," Jacobs said with an expression that almost made you believe she meant it.

"Sorry to run away but I have to get the auction started. If you want to bid on anything just raise your hand. If you win don't worry about payment tonight, just enjoy." And with that Caius walked off towards the Podium at the far end of the library.

Jack had noticed Caius's wine distributor quietly slipping away during the exchange. Caius's associates are loyal thought Jack. Few would risk offending Governor Jacobs by avoiding her questions. Jack was relieved the auction started as soon as Cereo reached the podium. Standing between Evans and Jacobs as they avoided even looking at each other was unnerving.

The auction was fun. Watching the wealthy bid against each other in sums that were meaningless to them was a lesson in local politics. The political, social, and business power structures were obvious after a few rounds. Jack watched carefully and took notice of who deferred to whom. The cold knot in his stomach returned after Jacobs and Evans started bidding against each other for the evening's last bottle. The colonist bidders withdrew immediately knowing their place.

Jack had recently learned enough about Arista wine to know the original vintage of Jenny's Acre was extremely rare. But as the bid price grew to an outrageous level he realized Jacobs was just playing with her food again. It ended as he thought it would. Jacobs deferred to Evans as it appeared he was becoming uncomfortable with the price. She gave him a respectful bow of her head acknowledging his victory and then turned her face away unable to hide a thin feral smile.

Senator Cereo walked over to congratulate Justice Evans. "Congratulations Justice. Your bid will feed a lot of hungry people. Your generosity is much appreciated. If you are a collector I would be happy to provide a signed certificate of authenticity. Believe it or not there have been fakes produced of this wine."

"I would appreciate that senator. While I would love to have a taste of it, I do have a collection of rare wines from across the Commonwealth. This will be given a special place in my cellar," Evans responded with a smile.

Later that evening they retired to what appeared to be the senator's expansive office. As they sat down to start their discussion Caius's valet entered with a bottle of Jenny's Acre and four glasses.

"I thought we might enjoy the same vintage you both bid on tonight. Justice Evans will know what he has in his wine cellar and Governor Jacobs will discover whether she should have bid higher. Seems like a way for everyone to win," Caius said with a smile.

Jack was floored. Given what the auctioned bottle had sold for this was beyond extravagant. Caius's observation that everybody wins wasn't lost on anyone. A perfect way to start the discussion. Evans was beside himself with glee. The senator was perfectly using one of the Justices weaknesses to manipulate him into a sense of obligation. An expensive but highly effective move.

Jack took a tentative sip of his wine and was surprised. He wasn't sure what he had expected. It was very smooth and dry with a subtle tart taste that flowed over his palette. While he wasn't a wine drinker, this was pleasing. Evans was using the situation to rub in his winning bid by effusively complementing the wine. Jacobs just watched him with that hidden smile of hers, privately pleased that she had manipulated him almost as well as Cereo had.

After Evans' complements tailed off Governor Jacobs kicked off the conversation. "You've invited us here so that the Commonwealth is aware of Arista's plans with regards to Liberty."

Caius smiled and then said, "we understand the Commonwealth wants to be informed of any plans that may affect tax revenues. You've been very clear that the Commonwealth has strict Edicts on non-interference in colony politics. In other words, the Commonwealth would like to be aware of plans and developments but will not take sides."

"I'm really pleased to have my faith in Governor Jacobs confirmed. There have been sector governors who have violated the non-interference Edicts. It's gratifying to work with a governor who sets a high ethical standard," Evans said while indicating the opposite with his tone of voice and body language.

At this point Caius jumped in and said, "let me outline the emperor's plans. First let me assure you that Emperor Trajan is very supportive of the Commonwealth being aware of his efforts. His goal is to increase the wealth of the Commonwealth. He believes the Commonwealth would be enriched if Liberty were as well managed as Arista. You are all aware of how segmented and divisive Liberty is today. The result of the current chaos is a lower standard of living for everyone. We even feel it here on Arista. To contribute to the welfare of the Commonwealth he intends on invading and subjugating Liberty. The plan is to separate the population into those who can lead and those who are most effective being told what to do. Any questions so far?"

"Assuming you are successful, is Trajan intending on changing the constitutional protections for the people of Liberty?" Evans asked.

"Trajan believes the bulk of the population's lives would be improved if they were slaves. It would be a transition from constant warfare and suffering to one of efficient societal contribution. Clearly a better result for the people of Liberty as well as the Commonwealth," Caius responded.

"You make it sound like Trajan is sacrificing for the Commonwealth. Clearly Arista has other goals in mind for such a large and risky investment," Jacobs said with a smirk.

Caius smiled knowingly back at Jacobs and said, "the emperor's plan is to expand Arista governance to include both planets. In addition to increased trade, the wealth of the two planets combined will be enhanced. Adding to the emperor's motivation is a personal desire to emulate his namesake. While personal goals are secondary to the wealth of Arista, and the Commonwealth, they do play a part."

"You currently have the queen of Liberty in your custody. What are your intentions? She is head of state for one of the Commonwealths colonies after all," Evans asked.

"What we have told Liberty is that we don't know who we can safely release her to. So, for her safety we await their resolution of who was to blame for her kidnapping. We believe this is what is best for the people of Liberty," Caius said. Then changing tone, he lowered his voice as if sharing a secret and said, "to be completely transparent, Trajan's real intent is to magnify their dysfunction. The goal is to force her to perform a subservient role after our invasion has been successful."

"Who was responsible for her kidnapping?" Evans asked sincerely.

"We really don't know," Caius said looking at Evans innocently. "It's a happy coincidence that it probably isn't safe to turn her over to anyone on Liberty until that is known."

"My understanding is that her servant is going to be turned over. How do you know that is safe?" Jacobs asked.

"She is a servant. On Arista a slave would perform her functions. We are not overly concerned with her safety. However, you are making an excellent observation. It was my recommendation that she be released as a good will gesture. The emperor decided we should ask Liberty to send a delegation to retrieve her. Best case it drives further division on Liberty, worst case we end up negotiating with both sides before our invasion."

Evans was nodding his head and said, "please keep me updated on developments. As you know the Commonwealth does not have jurisdiction over interplanetary politics. In fact, it is a violation of our founding Edicts to get involved." Evans swung his head to look directly at Jacobs and smiled coldly. It was an obvious accusation.

Caius nodded his head and said, "let me assure you that Arista is not asking for anything from the Commonwealth. We believe that keeping the Commonwealth abreast of plans and developments that could impact tax revenues are a responsibility of a well-managed colony."

As Caius walked them out to their carriages Jack reviewed the evening. He wasn't sure whether to be pleased or panicked. Julie was going to rip him to shreds by being surprised with Evans' attendance. 'Never let your superior be surprised' was an axiom to live by. On the other hand, Caius had played Evans perfectly. He had hidden their involvement in the scheme while justifying continued communication on the topic. Any follow-on meetings discovered by Evans could be explained as 'just getting an update'. Jack was so distracted with worry that he didn't even hear what Julie and Caius discussed on the way out. That was dangerous and he scolded himself to be more careful.

Once in the carriage and on their way Julie said, "Senator Cereo is much more impressive than I imagined. His manipulation of the situation was masterful. In one fell swoop he put us in our place while making sure Evans wasn't going to be a problem."

"My apologies for not anticipating this move. I should not have let you be surprised tonight," Jack said with his head slightly turned down in a submissive gesture.

"I wasn't surprised. I know everything Evans does. That's the reason I asked to join tonight. The senator is good, very good. He's proven to be everything you said and more. He would make an excellent First Minister," she said smiling in a way that indicated his performance in that role was marginal. "But don't worry, you have your value as well," Julie said in a soft and intimate but predatory tone while patting his arm. Clearly indicating his extracurricular activities partly made up for a lack of professional attributes.

His shivered inside for what seemed like the millionth time and said, "so we're going forward with Senator Cereo's plan."

"No Jack. He's too smart. Evans was surprised by my arrival, Senator Cereo wasn't. I will have to root out how he acquired my travel schedule. Cereo would be impossible to predict and control. Unless we find a weakness to exploit he's too dangerous. I admire him. But I've learned those you admire are the ones who can destroy you. Something is going to have to be done about his relationship with Evans. I'll handle that part. It's time for you to put pressure on Pluta and Trajan to get moving on a Liberty invasion. There isn't anything Senator Cereo can do if the emperor is supporting Pluta. Let's enjoy the evening and discuss tomorrow how you'll arrange an understanding with Trajan and Magistrate Pluta."

She was probably right. While Cereo could be a powerful partner, he was very dangerous. Pluta, also dangerous, was more predictable and thus easier to control. In thinking ahead to the rest of the evening Jack shivered once again. He would have to perform again tonight. He realized that the one thing he could honestly claim to have gotten out of working for the governor was a deep gut level empathy for those forced into prostitution.

CHAPTER 22

# THE DARK SECRET

Hestie was in the small library alcove where she enjoyed doing her genetics research. After Gloria had caught her looking at raw DNA code in the commons area she decided she needed to be more careful. Soon after arriving at the university, she had gotten lost looking for biological reference materials. She had wandered into a side tunnel of the natural cave system beneath the university library. She found herself amongst rows and rows of ancient history books that had decades, if not centuries, of dust on them. She was intrigued. Perusing this section of old title storage turned into a hobby for her when she needed a break. One day after a couple of months of random reading she discovered gold. In a back corner, buried in dust, and clearly mis-shelved, were three hardbound books. They were each very thick and contained nothing but human genome data. Hestie was in heaven.

She had immediately known it wasn't a complete genome. There were simply not enough pages for that. But with no title page, table of contents, or appendix she was lost trying to figure out what she had. She did finally crack the unusual notation code that identified where in the genome each of the documented sequences were located. It took weeks of study to realize that each book contained sequences from a different individual. Comparing the books she determined that they were focused on specific differences between the three individuals.

Then the fun began as she started to tease out what those

differences were. After much study It slowly began to take shape. Two had brown eyes and one had blue eyes. Two were female and one was male. One was dark skinned, one was light skinned, and the third was somewhere in between. One was tall and two were short. Two were slender and one was robust. All three had brown hair.

Today she was hit by a thunderbolt. She suddenly realized something that shocked her to her core. She sat for a long time before deciding what it meant. Then she had to determine what to do with the information. Should she just keep it a secret? Would people be angry with her? Had she broken the laws around genetics research? In the end she decided she needed to test her hypothesis with the one person on the planet who might be able to find a flaw in her logic. Her mother.

Her head was spinning as she walked from the library to the medical research building. She was lucky her mother was on one of her frequent trips to the university. Hestie found her in the office the university provided for her. She knocked on the door, entered, and closed the door behind her. Her mother just looked at her with owlish eyes and waited for Hestie to tell her why she had come. It would have been mildly rude if anyone else had done this. It didn't bother Hestie at all, this was her mother, and she loved her.

"Mom, I've been researching DNA for the past few months. I've stumbled on something confusing. Unless I'm missing something, it's also disturbing," Hestie said plainly.

"What did you discover?" Her mother asked.

Hestie always watched her mother closely. Growing up she had learned to discern emotions that were invisible to everyone else. Her mother was worried. This was a woman who was unnaturally calm even in the worst situations. Hestie swallowed, took a deep breath, and explained, "a few months ago, I found three hardbound books in the library archives that contain DNA information. After studying them I decided each of the three were different individuals and the books detailed their differences. Eventually I figured out that two of them were parents of the third. What was initially surprising was that the child had genes indicating it was much larger than the parents. I thought that odd and dug deeper. I discovered the child had higher bone and muscle density, larger lung capacity, and a larger heart. What I suspect is that this child mirrors current Pacifica humans while the parents appear to be from the original colonist stock. What is disturbing is that this change doesn't mirror micro-evolution over 40 or 50 generations. It's a single generation set of changes." Hestie stopped for a moment before concluding, "It suggests we're GEMs mom."

Her mother had gone from worry to shock. Hestie couldn't remember her mother ever being so distraught. Perhaps she was misreading her mother because she herself was so upset. Hestie watched her mother gather herself and finally ask, "How long have you been able to read the genome without guidance, a map, or notes."

Hestie turned a light shade of red. This was embarrassing she thought. Then she confessed. "Since you brought home the first genetics book from the library."

"Why didn't you tell me you could do this?" her mother asked.

"I was embarrassed," she admitted in a soft voice.

Then to Hestie's horror, her mother started to do something Hestie had never seen her do before. Her mother started to cry.

CHAPTER 23

# TRAJAN'S CHOICE

There was a light tap on the door dragging Pluta out of the financial details of his sprawling slave trading business. "What is it," he said in an angry voice. Pluta did not like being disturbed when he was buried in a business review.

Henry opened the door and said in a hushed voice, "Apologies sir. The First Minister is in the entry hall asking for an audience. Shall I tell him to come back another time?"

What does that weasel want now thought Pluta. It's clear the Commonwealth is backing Cereo, and I really don't have time for meetings with no purpose. He wanted to instruct Henry to tell Jack he would have to schedule an appointment sometime later next week. But, he took a deep breath and said, "take him to the library and tell him I'll join him in five minutes." Hesitating as a thought occurred, he flashed a spiteful grin and continued, "Henry, pull out a recent vintage of Jenny's Acre and offer him a glass. Pore me a glass as well and position the bottle so the label is visible to the First Minister."

"Yes sir," said Henry.

When his information network informed him that the Governor had attended a Dry Brook Vineyards wine tasting he was incensed. Caius had purchased the old Domus Cereo successfully through anonymous agents. It was galling that the governor had met with Cereo at a property that should still be his. He had been talked into letting it go because an offer had come in at twenty percent above market. His previous real estate manager told him he would never get a

175

better price for the old broken-down mansion. That man learned what happens when you disappoint Pluta. The wine will let Jack know that I am aware of the Governors' meeting with Cereo he thought.

"Welcome Jack, what a nice surprise," Pluta said with his false smile as he entered the library.

"Thanks for seeing me on such short notice Magistrate. I know you're a busy man," Jack said matching Pluta's phony smile with one of his own.

"Not a problem Jack, you are always welcome here."

"Your choice of wine for this occasion is appropriate. I wanted to discuss Senator Cereo and the results of a meeting the governor had with Emperor Trajan," Jack said as his smile faded and was replaced with a businesslike one.

So that's it. Jack has come to gloat. How immature. Just one more reason to try and break this puppy at some point thought Pluta. "I am always ready to do whatever the emperor desires. If that aligns with the needs of the Commonwealth all the better," Pluta said straining to keep his voice pleasant. He knew his façade was starting to crack and silently barked at himself to get under control.

"Trajan decided he wants to hear your ideas on the Liberty situation once more. As you know the Commonwealth really doesn't get involved in colony politics. However, the governor is supportive of your proposed plan to increase tax revenues," Jack said.

Pluta just stared at Jack in shock. He was sure he had been out maneuvered by Cereo. Speechless as he thought through the implications he finally said, "I'm glad the emperor has decided to hear more about my plan for Liberty. Did the Emperor have any additions or alterations to what has already been discussed?"

"He did discuss some ideas, but he wanted to deliver those thoughts to you personally. Since the emperor knew I was planning to visit this afternoon he asked me to relay his desire for an immediate audience," Jack said with a knowing smile. Jack took a final sip of his wine and said, "Excellent vintage. I'll have to procure some of this while I'm here." Then he stood and said, "I'll show myself out. The governor and I look forward to seeing progress." The comment about procuring Jenny's Acre caused a jolt of anger to hit him. That bastard really knows how to pull my strings. I need to stop underestimating him Pluta concluded.

Pluta waited until he heard the door close and then called out to Henry, "pull out my best suit and have the carriage brought around. I've got an appointment to see the Emperor. Move quickly." As he was getting ready to depart Pluta thought to himself, I really do need to do something about Jack.

Pluta was led under guard though the reception areas of the palace and eventually into the expansive central garden. He was guided down a series of stone walkways to one of Trajan's private alcoves. The central garden was a mix of large open areas and carefully hidden alcoves. The emperor was fond of picking these intimate alcoves for meetings with individuals. It was considered an honor to be invited to one. While Pluta had been to the large meeting area in the center of the garden many times, being invited to an alcove was a rare experience. This will put the bastard in the right frame of mind thought Trajan.

Pluta entered the small intimate garden and said, "good afternoon Your Eminence."

"Pluta, thank you for coming so quickly. It's a pleasure to see you," Trajan said smiling. The smile was a sham, which he didn't even try to hide. Trajan was wary of Pluta and his influence. While he had more confidence in Cereo, the governor had made it clear the Commonwealth preferred Pluta. It irritated him that they would interfere in his internal affairs. However, Tragen was a realist. He might be the undisputed ruler of this planet, but the Commonwealth could squash him like a bug if they decided they wanted him gone.

"I am at your command," Pluta responded.

"Review your plan for Liberty. I've heard it before but want to ensure I'm up to date," Trajan said.

Pluta brightened and reviewed the plan he had previously presented. "As I'm sure you'll remember, Lord Druango is eager to form a coalition with Arista to take control of the planet. He proposes maintaining the current monarchy. After victory is achieved he will ensure that Prince Justin is convicted and executed along with his extended family. That leaves Queen Olivia as the sole member of the royal family. He plans to marry the queen then force her to comply with his rule. Per Liberty's succession rules he would have to do that as Queens Consort. This has historical precedence in Liberty whenever the king or queen is unable to perform their royal duties. In return for assisting him he'll pledge a tribute equal to 60% of Liberty's share of the Commonwealth's increased tax revenues. He also pledges to remove natural rights clauses in their constitution. That will permit slavery to be legally practiced. He will also sign a treaty in which Arista will be given a license to manage all of Liberty's slave trade."

"Senator Cereo made some good arguments for making Liberty a region of Arista rather than a subject kingdom. Why isn't that a better plan?" Trajan asked in a tight voice.

Pluta quailed and was obviously trying to come up with an answer. After a long minute he said, "Legate Ricci believes our Legions will be three times the strength of the Liberty Rebel Army when the war ceases. We can decide then which system to enable. Perhaps we can convince Lord Druango to rid himself of the royal family and become governor of the planet rather than ruler," Pluta said smiling.

"Why wait. We have the upper hand here. General Eastbrook will put down the rebellion if they don't get help from us. Just tell Druango what his role is going to be. You're a businessman. You should know how to negotiate. I want Liberty to be a region of Arista and NOT a subject kingdom. Do you understand?"

"Yes Your Eminence," Pluta said clearly shaken.

"Good, good," Trajan said in a satisfied voice. "I have decided you will head up Arista's post war consolidation efforts. The military strategy and invasion will of course be handled by a Legion Legate. You will act as a consultant in those matters. I have grown impatient with Senator Cereo and expect you to do better. However, I like his plan better and expect you to deliver a new region to our rule and nothing less," Trajan said.

"I am humbled and pleased to perform whatever service you desire," Pluta responded with a true smile on his face. "Does Legate Ricci know of his role yet?"

Trajan gave a twisted and obviously satisfied smirk and said, "I have decided that Legate Vincentius Cereo will command the invasion. The 2nd Legion has been informed they are to proceed to Roma to await orders. They will spearhead the attack. The Commonwealth has agreed to supply transport immediately and can move one legion at a time. I am expecting you to move quickly." Trajan was delighted to see how uncomfortable Pluta was with this proclamation. Having Caius Cereo's eldest son head up the invasion would further divide the senate to his benefit.

Pluta took his time digesting this information and finally said, "I understand and will do whatever is necessary for success." He waited for Trajan to acknowledge his submission. With a head nod from Trajan, he continued. "Given the need for quick action I recommend Liberty's queen and her servant be moved to Roma under my protection. This will assist in accelerating negotiations with Druango and planning for post war consolidation."

"I'm leaving her where she is for now. She is isolated from Roma intrigues. I want to ensure that continues. We'll hold onto her until Liberty is mine. If all goes well she can offer me a little personal entertainment. After than perhaps she ends her days at the Arena. Everyone should witness her ultimate submission to my rule," Trajan said firmly.

"I will contact Lord Druango and get started immediately," Pluta said and started to rise up off his chair.

"Lord Druango is on his way to Arista as we speak. You and Legate Cereo will finish negotiations with him and submit a plan as quickly as possible." Trajan hesitated and then said, "the war will be over soon after we land our legions. You better ensure consolidation is done just as quickly" The implied threat was abundantly clear.

"Yes Your Eminence," Pluta said and then hurried off clearly shaken by the encounter.

It made Trajan smile to see Pluta terrified of him. Just another attribute of a weak blood line. Cereo would never show fear like that. Trajan sat for a while dreaming about his legacy. He would be a true namesake to the original Trajan. Liberty first and then Pacifica. Once those dominos dropped the other planets in the sector would be easy to add as well. There were two other sectors in the Commonwealth under the control of a single planet and Sector 27 was going to be the next. He smiled to himself imagining Pluta's reaction when he referred to the young Vincentius as cousin. He just hoped Cereo's son was as quick witted as his father and name him Trajan in return.

Frowning he thought through the challenges. He didn't trust Pluta, Druango, Cereo, or the Commonwealth. All of them want power and will rob whatever they can from my legacy. Best to keep them all guessing. Even assuming each does their part it doesn't guarantee success. He reflected once more that blood lines were important. He worried Pluta would not be up to the task. Oh well, he thought, if Pluta fails I can always fall back on Cereo. One way or another Liberty will be mine and then work can start on acquiring the rest of the planets in the sector.

CHAPTER 24

# NAVIGATION

Hestie turned to Quinn, smiled, and said, "match."

"Match," he agreed. Then with his cheesy grin he added, "I never get tired of doing these calculations. Especially when we're pushing the distance."

"Explain to me why we're even doing this," Hestie said with concern. Her passion was diving into the original colony ships' medical and biological databases. The technologies were incredible. She was awestruck by the lives they could improve, extend, and save. The upside for Hestie in discovering they were GEMs was being allowed to dive deep into the vast information resources of the original colonists.

Quinn's smile faded just a bit, and he said, "Professor Dacy says we have to be prepared to take advantage of a Commonwealth spaceship. He says we can't just give up no matter how bad it looks."

"But what is the probability of gaining control of a spaceship," Hestie said, Then she quickly raised both hands and added, "no don't tell me. If you do you'll have to explain how you arrived at your answer, and I'm not interested." Hestie smiled brightly at her brother. Quinn always made her smile inside and out. He was so uncomplicated. Of course, that actually made life complicated for him. Since he seemed unaware of the complications it was in reality a blessing. It was just good to see him so happy. People thought she was the one always helping him. The truth was that he helped her just as much, perhaps more.

They had been working on a navigation simulator for local wormhole jumps. These were temporary wormholes that could be artificially created. It involved extremely sensitive sensors that created an accurate 3D map of the far end of the envisioned wormhole. The sensors were the distance limitation. Since quantum computing was a required step a probabilistic result was the output. It was never perfect. Large amounts of computing time were required. As an additional safety factor each spaceship had two independent navigational mapping systems to calculate the wormhole construction. When their answers matched the likelihood of a mistake was near zero. It bothered Hestie that it was near zero and not zero. A mistake would place the other end of the wormhole somewhere in the universe better matching the model. You could end up anywhere with no path home. Of course, Quinn had no such reservations.

All of this took advantage of an epiphany in physics that had uncovered the mystery of gravity. With it a new standard model devoid of proxies like dark energy and dark matter. The old standard model was a grand accomplishment given the information available. But since adjustments to the theory had to be made every time a more sensitive telescope was deployed it was clear something was missing. It turned out that the early theories of quantum gravity were not quite right. The answer was quantum in nature, but not in any of the ways physicists had imagined for hundreds of years.

Allen's Law was actually named after a janitor. Allen was a savant with puzzles. His home was filled with intricate 2D and 3D cardboard, wooden, and metal puzzles he had collected and built over the years. It was rumored he could simply look at all the pieces laid out on a table and instantly know where each piece fit. To fund his obsessive-compulsive hobby, he took a job cleaning offices at CERN. One day while emptying a trash receptacle he asked CERN's director why everyone in the building was working on the same thing. Amused the director asked him why he thought it was all the same. The answer shook him to his core. Five years later, a large research team, which included Allen as a consultant, had worked out the math, performed measurements, and validated the theory. CERN's director refused to be named primary discoverer. He maintained until his death that Allen's insight was wholly responsible. His summary was "I just did the math." From this discovery interstellar and intergalactic travel was made a reality.

Hestie and Quinn were part of a six-person team required to operate the spaceship described in their simulator. Artificial Intelligence, AI, had almost destroyed humanity in the twenty-first century and limitations on computation were strictly adhered to. Those living through that horror had discovered that nuclear weapons weren't the biggest threat to humanity. The biggest threat to humanity was an AI enabled world wide web. Limitations could be broken down into three areas. The first prohibited AI algorithms from making decisions. Any decisions. The second was strict limitations on how computer systems communicated. Most systems were constrained to either send information and commands or receive them. Those who were allowed to have two-way communication were prohibited from having AI software of any kind. The third was limiting access to data for computing systems that utilized AI. Systems were designed for limited capabilities and only the data required for them to perform their function was allowed. Navigation was composed of three separate systems. First was plotting a desired path through local space. These systems had maps of the sector they were operating in. The second was a wormhole description, which Hestie and Quinn had just simulated. This system knew the vector math of the path but had no understanding of anything but the two points in space it was navigating between. The final piece of navigation was the wormhole generator. As far as the last two components of this system knew, they could be anywhere in the universe. Each of these three steps required human interaction and agreement. Redundancy of human judgement and manual data entry was the key to maintaining control. An autonomous self-aware computer-controlled spaceship was technically possible. History has shown the grievous mistake of allowing these types of systems to be created.

"My other question is why we are simulating a small warship?" Hestie asked.

"Professor Dacy says the only ship worth working on is one that allows us to fight. Everything else would be a waste of time," Quinn said while he looked away from her.

There it was again. A lie! Well maybe not a lie, but certainly he was withholding information. Quinn knew something he wasn't allowed to tell her. Oh well, she thought once again resigned to being in the dark. And it wasn't like she didn't have a secret she kept from Quinn. It was bad enough learning Pacifica natives were GEMs. What could possibly be worse than a death sentence. She was pretty sure she didn't want to know. That train of thought led her back to thinking about Jay. Her eyes still misted up when he entered her thoughts. It had been weeks since she last saw him and her despondency over their breakup wasn't getting any better. Perhaps worse. She had met him at the Blue Heron Tavern.

She had been procrastinating having the discussion and had talked herself out of doing it that evening. They were having so much fun and there was nothing she loved more than just hanging out with Jay. Then Jay said, "I think Tee is still alive."

"Really? Why do you think that?" Hestie asked, forcing a look of confusion on her face. She hated lying to Jay even if it was only a facial expression.

He looked at her with concern for a few moments and said, "Partially because you are keeping something about him from me. I know you. While you are good at hiding your thoughts, you can't completely fool me. I wouldn't press you on this if it was anyone other than Tee." Jay turned to the side to show her his first insignia and pointed to the thin red stripe on it. "This means he's always with me. It means I have an obligation to help him in any way I can. He's like a brother to me Hestie. More even."

Hestie's eyes teared up and she blurted out "I've been meaning to tell you this for a while. I've decided we are not a good match and it's better if we stop seeing each other."

He had just sat there staring at her for an uncomfortable couple of minutes before responding. "I don't believe you," Jay said with no malice on his face, only concern.

That was one of the things she loved about him. He was trying to understand her pain and grief instead of focusing on his own. Swallowing hard she said, "I've decided, it just isn't going to work." And then because she couldn't keep her emotions under control any longer she got up and hurried out. The last thing she heard as she was walking away from the table was Jay saying. "Something is going on. Just tell me and we'll figure it out."

She didn't respond. Diana sent her a letter a couple of weeks later asking, 'what the hell is going on with you and Jay'. Hestie didn't respond to that either. She couldn't think of anything to say. Diana was her best friend and knew her better than anyone. She simply couldn't come up with a story Diana would believe. She knew Jay was going to ask her to marry him. She would have said yes enthusiastically before the GEM discovery happened. It would have been a dream come true. But she couldn't say yes, she couldn't do that to him. She couldn't marry him and then kill herself without him knowing why she had done it. He would decide she had serious mental health issues that were hidden and breaking up with him was a symptom of that. She knew he would be sad at her death. It was much better this way for him, and for her.

CHAPTER 25

# TREATY

In the end Trajan couldn't resist toying with Lord Druango. Once the Commonwealth ship had landed Pluta had been summoned to the Palatium. Trajan sent a message informing him that Lord Druango was on his way for a meeting with the Emperor. Trajan wants to intimidate the poor bastard before discussions even start Pluta thought. He loves to scare the crap out of people and can't resist. Everyone except Cereo Pluta remembered. That thought peaked his hatred of the man. Trajan treats him like a long lost relative. Those thoughts were bouncing around in his head as he entered the central garden. Before he could greet Trajan Vincentius Cereo entered the garden on his heels.

"Hello cousin," Trajan said with a twisted smile moving his head to the side to look past Pluta as he greeted Vincentius Cereo first.

Vincentius hesitated, realizing the slight just given Pluta, and then said deferentially, "a pleasure to see you again Trajan."

Pluta's brain almost exploded. Bad enough the father was referred to as a family member but now the upstart Legate? The obviously pleased Trajan smiled back at Vincentius and then turned to Pluta frowning a bit. "Glad you found your way here Magistrate."

"At your command Your Eminence," he said respectfully, trying very hard to hide his outrage.

At that moment, an overweight, pasty looking man well

past his prime was led into the central garden by the First Minister.

Jack motioned the man to stand in front of Trajan and said, "it is my pleasure to introduce Lord Druango Your Eminence."

"Very pleased to meet you sir," Druango said.

"The proper way to greet me is by referring to me as Your Eminence, Your Majesty, or Your Primacy. Although that last one has fallen out of favor lately," Trajan said frowning.

"My apologies Your Eminence," Druango said haltingly. His demeanor going from confident to uncomfortable. Well, get ready to be even more uncomfortable thought Pluta smiling to himself.

"If it pleases Your Eminence I will retire and let the four of you discuss colony business," Jack said in a submissive fashion. What a suck up thought Pluta. But, I have to admit he does a good job of managing Trajan. Most Commonwealth citizens would treat him as someone of little regard. Jack seemed to understand the man had true power here on Arista which meant indirect power in the sector. Hard to use that power against a Commonwealth citizen, but it was power, nonetheless.

"Thank you for accompanying Lord Druango to my home. I understand you've found temporary quarters for him while he's here," Trajan said. Plura wondered if Lord Druango realized Trajan was insulting him. Anyone of significance visiting Roma was housed in the guest wing of the Palatium. It was a collection of elegant apartments meant to impress. It appeared that Trajan didn't care to impress the Lord.

Jack nodded his head in acknowledgement and said, "yes. I'll wait out in the reception hall for your meeting to conclude. Then I will accompany Lord Druango to his quarters. I'm sure he's exhausted from the trip."

Yeah, he sure looks like shit thought Pluta. This was

exactly the sort of man Pluta despised. Overweight, doesn't take care of himself physically, likely unable to defend himself. Obviously, a lazy man. Disgusting.

"Thank you First Minister. We appreciate all the support the Commonwealth gives to its colonies," Trajan said in an appreciative tone.

Jack gave a half bow and backed his way out of the garden. Acting like one of Trajan's subjects thought Pluta, further irritating him. Jack really was a man that shouldn't be underestimated.

"Tell me why you've come Lord Druango," Trajan said as if he didn't already know.

Druango hesitated, clearly confused. He gathered his thoughts and said, "I have a proposition for your consideration. Our offer will greatly increase the wealth of your kingdom Your Eminence."

"And what proposition is that?" Trajan asked.

"The queens uncle has rebelled against her succession to the throne by having her kidnapped and sent to Arista. I think he hoped I would be blamed for this. Instead, the House of Lords has declared him to be the culprit. Our army has cornered him, and we are asking for your assistance so that he can be quickly brought to justice," Druango said.

"And why should I care what happens on Liberty?" Trajan pressed.

Druango grew angry then and said, "You don't need to care. I have been negotiating with Overlord Bennett of Sector 3. General Harris, his top mercenary commander, is available. I just thought it would be better to keep this within Sector 27," he said defiantly.

"Come now Lord Druango. Do you think I'm an idiot? General Eastbrook is the one who has cornered you not the other way around. If you don't get immediate assistance your life is over. I know what kind of fees Bennett charges. You had better offer us something better than that."

"If you send two Legions back with me I will transfer 40% of the increased tax the Commonwealth has agreed to apportion to Liberty to Arista. A conservative estimate is at least five billion credits per year," Druango said smiling.

"Why don't I send three Legions and just take over the planet. Why do I need you," Trajan said in a thick voice leaning forward with his chin jutting out.

Sweat broke out on Druango's forehead, and he stuttered. "I was assured by the First Minister that you were in favor of an arrangement."

"The Commonwealth doesn't get involved in colony politics. It violates their non-interference Edicts. If I want to have you provide entertainment at our next Arena event they don't care. If I want to conquer Liberty and turn it into a slave planet the Commonwealth would just turn its head. I merely need to increase tax revenues. Which isn't hard if I control the planet," Trajan said in a tone that was just short of shouting. Lord Druango melted at that point. He was clearly terrified of Trajan and his eyes were darting wildly about looking for an escape. At that point Trajan barked out "Lord Druango." And when Druango eyes jerked back to him he said. "You are fortunate. I like having local governance for the regions of my empire. The First Minister and Magistrate Pluta seem to think you can effectively provide that. While I'm not yet convinced, I am willing to let you try and convince me. Before you ask about your fiancée' she is being well taken care of. I doubt we need royalty on Liberty, but just in case I'll keep her safe for now. Work with Legate Cereo and Magistrate Pluta on a plan to conquer and govern Liberty as a region of Arista. When you're ready to plead your competence request an audience." Then instead of dismissing him he smiled and said in a conciliatory voice, "Tomorrow you are invited to attend the Arena in my private suite. It's the first day of our New Years celebration. You might as well enjoy a little entertainment while you're here." After that announcement Trajan shooed them away.

As they exited the central garden Pluta was thinking it was

a little surprising the man hadn't had a heart attack. Or at the very least wet his pants. Trajan excelled at being rational one minute and unhinged the next. It kept a person guessing what was really going on. He hoped Druango was made of stronger stuff than was evident. In any case the man now knew his dreams of being the king of Liberty were over.

The following day Jack declined the emperor's invitation to attend the Arena. His excuse was that he had an important Commonwealth issue to deal with. Pluta didn't believe his excuse and it solidified his suspicion that Jack was soft. A weakness to be exploited perhaps. Lord Druango didn't realize that the Arena was more than gladiator bouts. The entertainment the emperor had mentioned the day before was much more gruesome than anything Druango had likely witnessed or even imagined. Pluta was really looking forward to watching Druango's reaction. At the last-minute Trajan had sent word that he would not be attending that day but wanted everyone to enjoy the festivities. Pluta knew this was twofold. First it insinuated that perhaps Trajan was working privately with Jack. If not it was clearly another insult. It was classic Trajan. Put people in their place and keep them guessing.

The day's activities started with an announcement of the first event. A man with a large megaphone walked out onto the sandy surface of the Arena floor to the cheers of the crowd and announced, "first up today is administering justice for dereliction of duty." A door opened up across from the emperor's suite and a nude man in chains was led out. He stumbled badly and instead of letting him get up was roughly dragged to a post, picked up and slammed against it. Then he was chained so that he had no choice but to stay upright. He sported a number of open sores and untended wounds all over his body. He had clearly been tortured. "This man was in charge of security on one of the Commonwealths transport ships. They were transporting slaves for Arista. He neglected to ensure that newly captured slaves were being properly secured. As a result, he was responsible for three guards and one highly valued slave being killed. These are the

190

four the Pacifica gladiator Tee murdered onboard ship." A roar of approval went up from the crowd when Tee's name was mentioned. The announcer waited for the cheers and applause to die down before continuing, "the slave Tee murdered was intended to be the one providing justice in the Arena. So, it's fitting that the murdered slave's replacement is the one to administer this judgement. In the meantime, since the murdered slave was originally requested by the emperor, this scum has been getting special attention from the Emperor Trajan himself." More applause. Then the announcer said, "let justice be served." As the announcer walked off a gaunt cruel looking man with various implements on his belt walked forward to the terrified cringing man chained to the post. The man started screaming before it even began.

Pluta couldn't remember the last time he had enjoyed himself this much. He had watched Lord Druango go from horrified to sitting frozen with a vacant look on his face. The best part was when he couldn't hold onto the contents of his stomach. It was clear Druango understood Trajan's threat to have him provide entertainment at the Arena was the same fate he was witnessing. He had gone into shock when the tortures grew more inventive, and eventually extremely personal. This was when the screams grew sharper and louder. When the screaming, sobbing, and begging weakened the man was told to beg for his death. A megaphone was held up to his ruined mouth so that the entire crowd could hear his plea. After the man made an impassioned plea the torturer decided to keep at it to the delight of the crowd. The torturer finally ended it when he sensed the crowd was growing bored. The rest of the day at the Arena was uneventful. Druango eventually decided to take advantage of the suites refreshments and drank himself senseless. He just sat and stared neither enjoying the gladiator bouts nor turning his head away at the more gruesome parts. Pluta was pleased. Lord Druango was now in the right frame of mind for negotiations.

Judgement

CHAPTER 26

# NEW YEARS FESTIVAL

Tee was holding his own against Victor. Then suddenly he wasn't. Lying on his back in the dirt Victor laughed and held his hand out to help Tee up.

"Don't feel bad Tee," Victor said with his smile still in place. "Even Griff doesn't know that trick. One of my failures is not completing Griff's training before I was kidnapped. One of the traditions of Master Sergeants was to withhold certain techniques until the person you're training as a replacement is considered worthy. With years to think about it I've decided this is a bad tradition. All Guard members ought to know all the tricks. For the Guard, important knowledge needed has likely been lost forever. If you get back to Pacifica I want you to promise you'll teach all the special techniques I teach you to Griff. Then make him promise to teach it widely."

"When we both get back to Pacifica we can share that duty," Tee said grinning.

Victor just looked at him oddly. Talk of getting back to Pacifica had started a few weeks ago when Tee told Victor, "I have an idea of how we might kill the emperor." As he said it he thought of Jay. Jay would smile and say it was just another suicide plan. Shaking himself out of his nostalgia he said in a low voice, "speaking of getting back to Pacifica, did Forti measure the wall yet?" Tee asked in a hushed whisper.

"Yes and you were right. It's almost the same height as the arrow and spear range barrier. Perhaps a bit less. Test out your idea tomorrow during practice. Don't be obvious Tee,"

Victor said in his mentor's voice while glaring for good measure.

Tee shot him his 'you don't need to state the obvious' look. Then he grew pensive keeping his eyes on the ground for a while. Looking up he said. "Do you really think this will work?"

"It all depends on whether you get in a kill shot quickly enough. I'm certain of giving you enough time for one but uncertain if you will have time to get off two," Victor said staring intently at Tee.

Tee stared back at Victor for a few moments and then said patiently, "I used to practice doing exactly this. Taking an unknown bow and executing a kill shot with the first arrow. I can get off a second arrow very quickly. I am confident of placing the second arrow where it's needed. Forti told me the bows used in the Arena match what I practice with. They are standard Legion issue. But they are not high-quality bows. There will be minor differences between them. I just don't know what those differences will be."

Victor huffed and said, "If nothing else it's a good plan. My idea of the two of us rushing the emperor's suite was doomed to failure. There are way too many security personnel around him and the archers placed on top of the walls would make pincushions out of us. Distracting everyone while you attack from across the Arena feels like something that might work. The people behind you will obviously see what you're doing, but surprise will give you some time. They will most likely panic seeing one of us on top of the wall. Forti will be in that general area along with a few others. That could buy us some time. As long as that bastard emperor dies, I'll go to my maker a happy man."

"Why is Forti helping us," Tee asked suspiciously. He had never quite gotten to the point of trusting the man. Much of that suspicion had to do with Forti working for Senator Cereo. How could he trust a man who thought he owned him, or anyone for that matter. He was also chummy with

Leo who Tee definitely didn't trust. There was something false about him.

"It's a sad story. He was a legionnaire who helped a slave girl escape. She had been assigned to him. It's one of the benefits given when a warrior reaches that status. She cooked, cleaned, mended his wounds, and provided company. After a few months he realized he was in love with her. It was impossible for him to buy her from the Legion. They don't allow the soldiers to have a future with the camp girls. They believe that would cause too many problems in the ranks. So, when she was scheduled to be rotated Forti helped her escape. The emperor himself got involved. One of the Legates mentioned the situation and the emperor decided to administer what he calls justice. They made Forti watch as the slave girl was tortured in the Arena. Then as they were dragging her dead body out his first match started. After Forti won Trajan announced that he was being given a chance to redeem himself because of his years of service to the Legion. Thirty hard fought bouts later he was a free man once more." Victor finished shaking his head. "The emperor is a monster. He needs to be put down. Don't worry about Forti, he's all in."

"I'm all in too Victor. Training to kill innocent people is not a life I care to continue. If we can provide some real justice it's enough for me," Tee said.

"Forti says there is a chance we can trigger a revolution. Everyone is terrified of the emperor but once he's dead they may be confident enough to throw down his government. The aristocracy is hated by most of the people of Arista. Citizens are a minority. I've told you what to say. Make sure you say it before you let go your first arrow. Make sure everyone around you hears it," Victor said sternly. "We have to spur them to action."

Tee smiled grimly. He didn't mind dying if he could protect others. If they could really kill the emperor then maybe the kidnappings and Arena atrocities would slow or even stop. If so, it would be enough.

The next day during archery practice Tee placed an arrow in the very top of the barrier. Eric had a ladder he used to retrieve these types of errant shots, but he wasn't around. Tee glanced around and up to the observation room. Seeing no one he casually walked over to the barrier and jumped. He caught the top of the barrier with one hand and then swung up to grab it with his other hand. He quickly pulled himself up and stood on top. He reached down and pulled out the errant arrow then jumped down. The other gladiators were staring at him. Damn, that wasn't inconspicuous at all he thought. Victor was glaring at him. Oh well, another lecture at dinner tonight. The good news was that jumping to that height was easy. He could get on top of the Arena wall anywhere he chose.

Standing back in the shadows of the observation room was Dobler. His jaw almost hit the ground when Tee did a standing jump and ended up on top of the barrier. The athleticism of the Pacifica gladiators was simply astounding. He never would have guessed anyone could do that. His eyes narrowed. But why? Why would Tee allow himself to be seen doing that? Was he testing an idea? Just then he realized the height of the barrier was similar to the height of the protective wall around the arena. Everyone thought it was plenty high enough to protect the spectators. This sudden realization made him smile. He knew he should report it. He knew that if something happened they would interrogate him and discover he had been holding back. If so, he might end his days as Arena entertainment. But every time he thought about giving a report the memory of the girl who looked so much like his daughter reappeared. Victor and Tee are good people he thought. Victims like himself. He would wait and see what happened. The next time they would appear in the Arena was New Years. They pulled out all the stops for New Years and both would definitely play a part. It would be just like Trajan to have them fight some ridiculous number of gladiators together. Perhaps he would buy a ticket this year.

As the New Years Ascension holiday drew nearer Victor's training grew even more intense. Lately Victor was a maniac.

There was a new technique almost every day and he was expected to do them perfectly. Tee took his lumps and learned. He wondered how he might fare against Jay these days. Those bouts had always been decidedly one sided. His confidence had grown from the months of training with Victor. He believed his new skills might even test Jay. That would be fun.

"Ok, that's enough for today." Victor finally said as daylight began to dim. "Tomorrow we do a light workout to loosen up and then rest. Let's have dinner and discuss the plan again. I want to make sure we both know what to do in various situations," Victor announced with a light sweat showing. It used to be that Tee was the only one sweating. The fact Victor worked up a sweat sparring with him was all the validation Tee would ever need. While he lost all the bouts, he was making Victor work and that was something to be proud of.

Dinner that night turned into a quiz session. Tee knew all the answers, but Victor wanted to hear them from him one more time. Tee had seen this behavior before when Victor was anxious. Tee guessed his obsessive nature was one of the things that made Victor special. His preparation was incredibly detailed with multiple backup plans. If they failed it would not be because of a lack of planning.

As they were finishing dinner Victor said, "make sure you shout out the call for revolution before you let the first arrow loose."

Tee rolled his eyes and in an exasperated voice said, "for heaven's sake Victor. You've told me that five times today. I think it's more important to see him dead than worry about starting a revolution. Yes, I'll make sure I say exactly what you taught me."

Victor stared daggers at him and said, "just make sure."

New Years Day morning came, and Tee had been too nervous to sleep. Was he nervous or already feeling guilty about the men he would be forced to kill today? Perhaps a combination of both. His expectation was that sleep wasn't going to matter after today anyway. Looking out his window as the sun was rising he was thinking about Grammy. She would tell him to fully enjoy his last sunrise. So that was what he was attempting to do. The beauty of the sunrise got him to think about Diana and the many shared sunsets and moon rises they had seen at the beach. He missed his family and friends terribly, but her most of all.

As the gloom started to fade into light he noticed Victor sitting across from Forti at one of the training ground tables. They were both leaning forward and having an intense conversation. How did Victor get permission to be in the yard that early? Tee was distrustful of Leo and Forti. He hoped Victor hadn't been taken in by a story of freedom invented by a slaver. Perhaps their plan was known to the emperor and was part of today's entertainment. He trusted Victor completely. He would just have to hope Victor wasn't trusting someone he shouldn't. His only worry should be doing his part exactly as planned. It would feel good to have a bow in his hand with something other than practice arrows. It would be especially satisfying to have the chance to dispense justice.

Victor had told Tee what their strategy would be if they fought together. It was similar to what Jay and Tee had used early in recruit training. Victor would go on the offensive and Tee would watch his back. However, what they had practiced was vastly more intricate than what he and Jay had done. His training in these techniques had been done in the evenings in Tee's cell. Victor didn't want the other gladiators to know how they would coordinate. Before Tee had explained his plan to Victor he had been intense with his training. Tee realized later than it was anxiety more than anything else. Victor remained an uncompromising taskmaster, but he seemed confident in their new plan. At least someone thought it might work.

Victor explained what he had learned just that morning as they were led into the tunnel for the Arena. "Forti told me the plan is to swarm us with a mix of gladiators, newly acquired slaves, and criminals. He wasn't sure how many would be released or when. The newly acquired slaves might be captured warriors from another world. What this means is that we have to focus on identifying and taking out the best fighters early. They will try and hide in the crowd to get close. They may even have a coordinated plan."

"How sure are you of Forti's information?" Tee asked.

"I'm confident of Forti. He's confident of his information. That's all you need to know," Victor said sternly, obviously irritated with Tee's continued suspicion of Forti.

"I will do my part Victor," Tee said with steel in his voice.

"I'm confident of that," Victor said softly. There was something approaching affection in his voice. He recovered his usual gruff manner and added, "just like we practiced. It's a dance and I'm leading. Watch my back but keep me in your peripheral vision. I may suddenly move at any time in any direction. You must stay positioned to protect me from what I can't see."

Tee swallowed a deep sigh and thought, he's told me this almost as many times as he's mentioned making the call for revolution before my first arrow. Well, I have to admit it's burned into my brain at this point.

As they arrived at one of the gladiators' doors to the Arena they heard the announcer say, "A special treat for your New Years enjoyment. We are recreating the Battle of Thermopylae. Playing the part of the Spartans will be the Pacifica gladiators. Perhaps Sparta will be victorious this time. Perhaps history will be repeated."

With that introduction the door opened, and Victor and Tee walked out. He noticed Victor's swagger and affected one for himself. The crowd did have an effect, and he smiled to think his ego might be getting a bit inflated. They had brought in large boulders and sprinkled them around on both sides of a wall they had built bisecting the arena. It did give the appearance of a narrow mountain pass. It had an opening just wide enough that Victor and Tee standing side by side could easily defend it. Thermopylae indeed. Victor and Tee walked over in front of the emperor's suite and did their customary roman salute. Then they both declared in unison, "for the honor of Emperor Trajan."

Trajan shooed them away with a limp wrist and bored expression. They jogged over and positioned themselves to protect the opening in the wall. Victor was actually smiling as he said, "This helps our plan as long as the main attack comes from the emperor's side. And that egomaniac will want the best view so that's guaranteed. We stay here until the bodies pile up and the flow of new warriors diminishes. When the doors open behind us we start our dance. At my signal you retreat to the far side. Be defensive, be boring, we need everyone to focus on me. I'll do everything I can to draw the crowd's attention. When I think the time is right I'm make my declaration and then you do your part."

"Tee grinned back at him and said in a sing song voice, "and I'll make my declaration before I loose the first arrow." They both chuckled.

"As all the doors on the emperor's side of the Arena opened Victor said, "it's truly been an honor Tee." And before Tee could respond insanity arrived.

After months of training Tee thought he had a good grasp of Victor's abilities. What he was witnessing was something else entirely. His speed, agility, and ability to kill with a single sword thrust was amazing. It also became obvious that he could pick out who was dangerous regardless of how they tried to blend in. Several times Tee had to lecture himself to stop being a spectator. He had a job to do. It was hard not to just watch the legend at work. As predicted, bodies started to pile up. Victor had been grabbing the dead and dragging or throwing them into positions that helped slow the main attack. He was building a wall of bodies. The fighting slowed and then stopped. Quiet filled the arena until the doors underneath the emperor's suite opened once more and a new mob of fighters emerged.

Victor grunted and said, "I'm guessing this is day two. If so, we won't have anyone attacking from behind until the next set."

"I'll keep watch," Tee managed to say before the next wall of fighters hit them.

After the fighting started to diminish once more Tee heard the crowd gasp. He turned his head to see a handful of gladiators pour out behind them. "Looks like they shortened it to two days," Tee said. Victor signaled a progression to their original tactic. Victor was the aggressor with Tee protecting his back. With both tiring and dripping with sweat the number of gladiators started to diminish. There were just two behind the wall now and a dozen or so trying to get over the dead body barrier. Victor had manipulated the action to get this result. He then signaled Tee to separate.

Tee turned his attention to the two remaining on their side of the wall. Out of the corner of his eye he saw Victor run and leap over the bodies piled in the doorway and then lost sight of him. From the swell of crowd noise, he guessed there was quite a bit of carnage going on. Neither of the two he was fighting had much skill. One was young, younger than anyone should be in the Arena. The boy was clearly panicked and was not thinking clearly. He had no skills but was pushing forward regardless. The threat of ending up as special entertainment at the Arena was a powerful motivator. The other was a middle-aged man who had some skill with the sword, but not much. It was easy to manipulate a quick retreat to the back side of the arena just under the far side archers' station.

The stadium had archers stationed every fifty feet along the periphery of the wall. They were not expected to get involved in the Arena battles. They were window dressing to make the spectators feel safe. Tee glanced up and the archer was intently watching the battle on the other side of the wall. Victor must be just underneath the emperor's suite by now. All of a sudden the crowd was cheering wildly. Then the mood completely changed with the crowd quieting and then they let out a collective gasp. All of the archers started notching arrows with their eyes locked on the other side of the separator wall. Victor must have made his declaration.

Tee didn't hesitate. He killed the older more skilled attacker and slammed his shield into the adolescent knocking him to the ground. At least that death won't be on my conscious he thought. Dropping his shield and sword he jumped, grabbed the top of the wall, and in seconds was standing on top, right next to the archer. The man who had been ready to fire an arrow was stunned to look up and see Tee towering over him. He just stared dumbly as if he couldn't believe what he was seeing. Tee grabbed the man's tunic with one hand, pulled the bow away from him with the other. Then he tossed him off the wall. He felt good that perhaps this man would live as well. Broken bones perhaps, but a chance to live. All hell was breaking loose around Tee as the crowd scrambled in panic to get away from him. Tee stepped to the arrow stand and quickly selected two arrows. He notched the first and as he pulled back, he turned, looked up, and located the emperor. Trajan was still sitting down and looking wide eyed down below. He imagined Victor was causing enough havoc to captivate him. Out of his peripheral vision he saw the other archers letting loose their arrows. He caught himself and hesitated long enough to loudly shout his declaration before letting the arrow loose. He mentally thanked Victor. He had almost forgotten to do that with all the chaos. With the first arrow on its way he quickly notched the second. He had known almost immediately that his first arrow was at least three or four inches too high. Wincing internally, his thoughts went to his mother. She would be disappointed with that shot. Although he heard movement behind him he took an extra moment to make sure of his aim and let it loose. He had a moment of satisfaction knowing this arrow was flying true. Then his world went black.

# ABOUT THE AUTHOR

Tom Burrell resides with his wife in Northern California. When not writing, Tom is busy with their five children and five grandchildren. He has a degree in mechanical engineering from Cal Poly San Luis Obispo. Before becoming an author, Tom enjoyed a career in the electronic test and measurement industry.

Prior to becoming a responsible adult, Tom spent a decade of his youth wandering aimlessly working a long list of jobs. These included lifeguard, swimming instructor, janitor, security guard, grill cook, painter, greenhouse worker, midnight shift convenience store clerk, residential liquor delivery driver, waiter, too many factory jobs to count, day laborer when immediate cash was required, and maker of handmade deer skin cowboy hats. These custom hats were sold by traveling around California to county fairs and other events where people tend to drink too much.

If you enjoyed Pacifica please consider giving a review. Feedback is a generous gift.

Book 3 of The Revelation Trilogy will be released in the fall of 2024.

Made in the USA
Columbia, SC
04 November 2024

45403062R00126